"Can't you trust me, just for a little?"

But Katya's heart was pounding, and she felt very cold. "I did trust you! You've been telling me what a bad influence my grandparents are, Matt, but they haven't tried to keep me in a fool's paradise while they manipulated me." Her voice broke.

"Things aren't as they look." Matt was white about the mouth. "You know what your grandparents have done to you and to your cousin—"

"You're in no position to criticize," she said bitingly. "*They* haven't lied to me."

"There are lies and lies," he said sadly. "You sit there and accuse me of things that happened ten years ago that you know nothing about. The real laugh is on me for thinking there was a real woman under that exquisite aristocratic face of yours."

He took her face between his hands and stared down at her as if he barely recognized her.

SOPHIE WESTON wrote and illustrated her first book—
at the age of five. After university she decided on a
career in international finance, which was tremendously
stimulating and demanding, but it was not enough.
Something was missing in her life, and that something
turned out to be writing. These days her life is complete.
She loves exciting travel and adventure yet hates to stray
too long from her homey cottage in Chelsea, where
she writes.

Books by Sophie Weston

HARLEQUIN PRESENTS
838—EXECUTIVE LADY
870—A STRANGER'S TOUCH
918—LIKE ENEMIES

HARLEQUIN ROMANCE
1925—BEWARE THE HUNTSMAN
2005—GOBLIN COURT
2129—WIFE TO CHARLES
2218—UNEXPECTED HAZARD
2362—AN UNDEFENDED CITY

These books may be available at your local bookseller.

Don't miss any of our special offers. Write to us at the
following address for information on our newest releases.

Harlequin Reader Service
901 Fuhrmann Blvd., P.O. Box 1397, Buffalo, NY 14240
Canadian address: P.O. Box 603,
Fort Erie, Ont. L2A 9Z9

SOPHIE WESTON

shadow princess

Harlequin Books

TORONTO • NEW YORK • LONDON
AMSTERDAM • PARIS • SYDNEY • HAMBURG
STOCKHOLM • ATHENS • TOKYO • MILAN

Harlequin Presents first edition December 1986
ISBN 0-373-10942-3

Original hardcover edition published in 1986
by Mills & Boon Limited

CHAPTER ONE

'So here you are,' said Dmitri Kolkanin, heavily jovial and not quite managing to hide his disapproval. 'Antisocial as always, Katya?'

'Yes,' Katya said absently, not looking at him. Across the room the stranger who had been watching her all evening had turned his head.

Dmitri frowned. 'You were not there to be introduced to the Ambassador.'

'I was looking at the display of icons,' Katya said without noticeable contrition. Who *was* he? she thought as the unknown man met her eyes yet again. She could not make out his expression, though she could see that he was not smiling. It chilled her slightly, that steady, unselfconscious regard. She turned impulsively to Dmitri to ask him whether he knew the man, but Dmitri had already embarked on a reproachful speech.

'It is a great honour for us to be asked to dance here this evening, you know. After all, we are only amateurs. And when the Ambassador was kind enough to spare us a few minutes, I found it very embarrassing to have to tell him that Mademoiselle André was the youngest and newest member of the group and I didn't know where she was.'

Katya chuckled suddenly, looking up at him with mischief. 'I expect he thinks I'm a security risk after a build-up like that,' she told him cheerfully.

Dmitri was appalled. 'That is not an amusing joke,' he said stiffly. 'It is in very poor taste, in fact. We will forget you said it.'

Katya sighed. Dmitri Kolkanin was a kind and protective man who had taken her under his wing when she first arrived from London and Paris was dauntingly strange. Her Russian ancestry was a passport to the informal Russian Club which met twice a month and where he taught folk dancing and Russian conversation classes. Dmitri had introduced her, helped her to find somewhere to live not too far from the university and, eventually, allowed her to join his precious dancing group. She was grateful. She was even fond of him. But she could not pretend that as a companion he was anything other than a crashing bore.

He was handsome enough, in a heavy-browed, burly way, thought Katya, considering him under her lashes. Not of course to compare with the stranger she had caught staring at her. Now he was unforgettable. He was very tall with a head of Venetian-red hair that would have got him noticed even if it hadn't been for the impossibly handsome bone structure or the faint unmistakable aura of sensuality that Katya could pick up at twenty yards across a crowded room. He was not, of course, alone.

She said suddenly, impulsively, 'Dmitri, do you know that couple over there?' She nodded in his direction. 'The girl in white with the very tall red-haired man. I keep thinking I've met them somewhere.'

Dmitri looked, not very interested. 'That is Steffy Solomon, the film star,' he said after a moment. 'Do you not recognise her?'

He was faintly incredulous. The actress was famous, elegant and much publicised. She was also, having just finished filming in France, the current darling of Paris.

Katya shook her head. 'I've heard of her, of course, but I've never seen one of her films. And I can't afford *your* sort of magazines, so I've never seen a photograph of her,' she teased. Dmitri was a photographer, his flat always overflowing with copies of the glossy magazines that bought his work. 'And the man?' she added idly.

'You spend too much time cooped up in your room writing that miserable thesis of yours,' Dmitri remonstrated. 'It is not natural for a young girl. You *should* have seen one of her films, instead of working all hours God sends. I will take you to see *Laredo* next week.'

'Thank you,' said Katya with restraint. 'Will the man be in it as well?'

Dmitri looked casually across the room again and gave a snort of laughter. 'You really *are* out of touch, aren't you? He's not a film star, that one, he's . . .'

But an attaché was beside him, murmuring in his ear. Would he come and look at the area of the room they had cordoned off for the dancing display? The Ambassador's wife was wondering whether it was big enough. With a brief nod to Katya, Dmitri allowed himself to be led away.

She stared after him, frustrated and slightly amused. Dmitri was a walking encyclopaedia of knowledge on the famous and talented, particularly those thronging the American Embassy's reception tonight. Now she would have to wait, have to remind him, before she could find out who it was who had been watching her with that curious, speculative intentness.

Of course, he could have been scrutinising her because he fancied her, Katya thought wryly. She collected a glass of cold wine from a passing waiter and began to stroll round the room, looking at the collection of Russian miniatures on the wall. She sipped. No, she didn't think that the stranger had fancied her. For one thing she had few illusions about herself, she knew she was not in Steffy Solomon's league. For another, that was not the *way* he had looked at her. Katya knew the way men looked if they were attracted, for all that she kept them at arm's length. It was unmistakable. She knew the look—

speculative, good-humoured, faintly questioning. The
tall stranger had not looked at her like that. He had
looked at her as if he could not believe his eyes; as if
he recognised her and, moreover, would much rather
not have recognised her.

She shrugged faintly, moving on. It must be her
imagination, the Russian taste for melodrama that ran
so deep in her family—though generally she herself
did not succumb to it. To her grandfather's disgust,
she recalled, half-smiling. He could not bear it when
she stayed calm under one of his rages.

The smile froze on her lips as a voice behind her
said, 'Good evening, Princess.'

For a moment she was rigid. Nobody in Paris knew
her full name, let alone her title. She did not recognise
the slow husky tones with their faint flavouring of a
Transatlantic accent. And yet she did. She turned
slowly.

'I'm not mistaken, am I?' Close to he was
breathtakingly attractive; and the cool grey eyes knew
they were not mistaken. 'Princess Katerina
Andreyevna?'

Katya met the unwavering, flinty stare with a slight
flip of her heart.

'You know me?' she asked slowly.

He shook his head. 'Alas no, Princess. Though I
believe we did meet once, many years ago. I used to
know your grandfather in London and your cousins.'
He paused and added deliberately, 'You resemble your
cousin, Princess Irena, very closely.'

Katya winced. She knew only too well that she
looked like Vonnie. The whole family had been telling
her that ever since she was eighteen. The trouble was
that Vonnie, her grandfather's favourite, had made a
disastrous marriage and a worse mess of her
subsequent love life, so resembling Vonnie was no
great advantage. Particularly when Grandpapa, at his
most despotic, had announced that he was not going to

have a second grandaughter living alone and going to the bad. So Vonnie was a slightly dangerous subject.

She said, 'Are you a friend of my cousin's?'

The smile quirked. He had a long, mobile mouth which was as expressive as a shrug. Katya found herself wondering if he was an actor.

'Not of Princess Irena's, though I have met her. But I know Sergei and I was at Oxford with Paul.'

Katya relaxed a little. Paul was the oldest of her cousins and in some ways her closest ally in the family. He too was accused of being too Anglicised by their grandfather. He too was phlegmatic, unfeeling, boring, superior, and all the other adjectives that the old Prince liked to fling at them when they were trying to persuade him not to buy a palace or sail round the world single-handed. Paul had supported her when she said she wanted to go to university, and had helped her when she was offered the chance to teach and do her doctorate in Paris.

Now she smiled at the stranger—not with un-shadowed friendliness, for she was still inexplicably wary of him, but with cordiality. Paul's name was a passport to her good will, at least.

'Did Paul tell you I was in Paris?'

'I haven't seen Paul for—er—some years,' he said.

She raised her brows.

'Really? And yet you recognised me at a hundred paces? You must have a very good memory for faces, Mr—er?'

'Saracen,' he supplied, looking amused. 'And Princess Irena is very striking.'

'Yes,' Katya agreed despondently.

Though her resemblance to Vonnie was the bane of her life in the family battles in which she was constantly engaged, it was only a shallow likeness. She had the same high cheekbones and wide violet eyes, but there the resemblance ended. Vonnie was always golden brown from some recent holiday, while Katya's pale skin would not take the sun. Vonnie's face was a perfect cameo oval, while Katya's chin was stubbornly pointed and made her look, particularly when locked in combat with her grandfather, like a militant elf. And above all, she did not have Vonnie's full, sensuous mouth that made her cousin always look as if she had just come from some private assignation where she had been thoroughly kissed. As, Katya would admit fair-mindedly, she probably had more often than not.

She added defiantly, 'Though Vonnie's taller than me. And older.'

The look of amusement deepened. Katya was already blushing pink, hearing how catty that last remark sounded.

'Of course,' he was saying soothingly. 'But we were both younger by several years when I last saw Princess Irena.'

Katya fought down the blush and strove for composure. Whatever else had been left out of her education—and according to her schoolteachers when her family finally loosed her into the classroom it was altogether too much—Grandmama had instilled unforgettable lessons on social deportment.

'What did you study at Oxford?' she asked now in the voice her grandmother had taught her—'interested, my dear, but not inquisitive: one must never seem *eager*, it is very bad manners'—to use on such occasions. 'Are you a lawyer like Paul?'

He shook his head. 'No, I read music.'

'Music?' That startled her. He did not look like a struggling musician, he looked like a prosperous businessman or lawyer; like Paul, in fact. She smiled, 'I thought all musicians starved in garrets.'

He smiled back, his eyes looking warmly and directly into hers, bringing back that prickling sensation. Her lashes fluttered nervously.

'Oh, they do,' he assured her, 'it's part of the job

description. I've done it in my time and, believe me, the garret was so barren you would not have got a self-respecting church mouse to make a stopover in it. But eventually you graduate. These days I play piano for the rich and famous.'

There was a faint bitterness underlying the laughing tone, Katya thought. She looked at him enquiringly but his face betrayed nothing more than mild self-mockery. Perhaps it had been her imagination, again lacking her family's characteristic ability to turn every incident in their own lives into a drama, Katya was aware that she tended to detect drama in other people's lives where it probably didn't exist.

'Are you playing tonight, then?'

There was to be an entertainment later, after the speeches. That was why she was here. The Russian Club was putting on a display of national dance. Dmitri had grudgingly allowed that Katya was now good enough to make one of the troupe.

Her companion shook his head.

'Nope; my concert's next week. I've given up playing for free. I'm here strictly to get my photograph in the papers.'

No, it was not her imagination. There was real bitterness there, buried deep perhaps under the flippant manner, but still there. Katya's interest quickened.

'And will you get it? Your picture in the papers, I mean?'

He shrugged. 'I guess so. The guys were round with the cameras when we arrived. And Steffy's very photogenic.'

Katya's eyebrows flew up at the disparaging tone.

'You sound as if you don't approve.'

Again the shrug and the charming, lop-sided smile.

'It's nothing to do with me, Princess. That's the way these guys choose to make a living. Steffy likes to be photographed and it doesn't do me any harm.' He

gave a soft laugh. 'It may even do me some good, at
that. Piano players are ten a penny, but a piano player
who escorts Steffy Solomon—now that's something
different.'

Katya stared at him, half-affronted, half-surprised.
Grandmama would definitely not have approved of
this conversation. For one thing he seemed to be
moving fast on to a far too personal plane; for another,
his remarks were bordering on the insulting to the
lady he was, by his own account, escorting.

He said, 'Don't look so horrified, honey.'

The casual endearment jolted her, as she suspected
it was meant to.

She said, 'Are you *sure* we haven't met before, Mr
Saracen?' and even as she said it realised who he had
to be. 'You're Matthew Saracen,' she breathed.

It seemed to her that he tensed, that the look he sent
her was almost hostile.

'So?'

'I'm sorry,' she apologised in confusion. 'I should
have recognised you sooner. I wasn't thinking.'

He relaxed. 'No reason why you should. People
don't. And—in spite of any impression I may have
given you to the contrary—that's the way I like it.
Turning up this evening as Steffy's poodle wasn't my
idea. It was my agent's. I guess,' he added
thoughtfully, 'tickets aren't going well.'

He didn't sound particularly disturbed at the
reflection, Katya thought.

'What are you playing, Mr Saracen?' she asked. She
was genuinely interested, but it came out just as if
Grandmama had said it.

He had caught the intonation too; gracious, regal
almost, an anachronistic legacy from the days when
Grandmama expected at any moment that she and her
brood would be recalled to a restored Imperial court.
He grinned but answered straightforwardly, 'Mozart C
minor; Bach; and Chopin for the locals. Plus a modern

piece which nobody will listen to.'

'Then why play it?'

'I like it.' He met her eyes squarely. 'Don't you ever do things just because you like doing them, Princess? Or does everything in your life have to be commissioned and paid for in advance?'

No, Grandmama would certainly *not* have approved.

'I don't understand you, Mr Saracen,' Katya said distantly.

'Matt,' he corrected. 'And you do understand me, Princess. You're as bright as a diamond and I think you understand me very well.'

Katya was bewildered and hid it behind an air of hauteur that would have both astonished and impressed her grandmother had she been present to witness it, instead of plying her interminable crochet in the stuffy London flat.

'I am a research chemist, Mr Saracen,' she emphasised the formal title just a little, 'I am not a creative artist. Therefore I do not work to commissions.'

Matt Saracen gave a crack of laughter.

'All women are artists. And the art is—what shall we call it?—extortion? Emotional extortion?' The beautiful mouth thinned and the grey eyes hooded at some bitter memory that Katya could only guess at. 'It's a natural talent your sex possesses, and I don't suppose research chemists are any different from the rest of the tribe.'

She shook her head, too startled to be offended. She looked at the glass in his hand.

'Have you been at the party long this evening, Mr Saracen?'

'What?' The eyes lifted; she saw him come back, slowly, from whatever unhappy place he had been visiting. 'About an hour, I guess. Why? Oh——' as he saw the direction of her glance, 'I'm not drunk, Princess, not yet, anyway. I probably will be later, unless my agent gets to the waiters,' he added. 'And whether I'm drunk or sober I still tell the same story.' He lifted his glass and toasted her mockingly. 'I'm just more fluent when I'm tight.'

Katya found that she was faintly alarmed and decided that the only thing to do was to admit it.

'You terrify me,' she said crisply. 'You're more than I can handle in your present state of tongue-tied sobriety.'

He laughed again, but differently this time, as if she had surprised and amused him. She saw he was looking at her in a different way too, without that latent hostility, as if he had suddenly noticed her and found her interesting.

'I doubt that. You're pretty cool, Princess. I'd say you could handle anything that comes your way.'

Katya gave her low, husky chuckle, suddenly at ease with this man.

'That's what my grandfather says. Only he doesn't mean it as a compliment,' she told him wryly.

'Prince Casimir?'

'Oh, do you know him too?' Katya was slightly surprised. Paul didn't visit his grandparents often, and when he did seldom brought his friends. It was a long-standing bone of contention. Grandpapa thought that as head of the family he was entitled to vet the acquaintance of his grandson and heir; and anyway, as Katya irreverently reminded him, he was compulsively inquisitive about other people's private lives.

'Again, we've met,' Matt Saracen said uncommunicatively.

Katya smiled. 'Then you'll know that he likes his women emotional and expansive. I'm a great disappointment on both counts.'

He looked interested. 'No scenes?'

Katya shook her head sadly, her eyes dancing. 'No scenes,' she confirmed.

'That must send Prince Casimir into culture shock,' observed Matt dispassionately. 'What happens?'

'I had an English grandmother on my mother's side,' she explained. 'My grandfather puts it down to that. He's never really got on with the English.'

'But he's lived there for most of his life,' pointed out Matt, betraying a surprising knowledge of the Andreyev ménage for one who claimed to be a mere acquaintance, though Katya did not notice that until later.

'Has he?' asked Katya drily.

'But surely the flat in Campden Hill Road—They haven't moved, surely?' he said, looking disconcerted.

'No,' she agreed. 'But have you been to the flat?'

His mouth tightened again, almost as if he were in pain, but he said evenly, 'A long time ago.'

She shrugged dismissive shoulders. 'It wouldn't have mattered if it was in the nineteen-twenties. It doesn't change and neither do my grandparents—wherever they live is a little bit of Russia. And not just Russia; Imperial Petersburg.'

Katya could not avoid the recollections that flooded back. The flat was dark, shadowed by the buildings on the other side of the narrow street and by the old trees that grew outside the window. It wasn't small, but the profusion of objects with which her grandparents surrounded themselves made it seem so. There were small tables covered with heavy silver-framed photographs, too many heavy brocade chairs and sofas designed for a more gracious setting, pictures, icons, old carved chests full of heirloom linen kept in lavender for marrying granddaughters—she broke off her thoughts; that was not a path to follow. They had only two granddaughters, one who married too often and to the wrong people, one who had set her face against marriage at all. They were disappointed in their granddaughters and missed no opportunity to say so.

He had watched the shadow cross her face. Now he said gently, almost as if he understood what she was feeling, knew what she was remembering, 'Bit claustrophobic?'

She shrugged, not answering. A diplomatic reception was no place to discuss the tragedy of her childhood, especially not with an unpredictable stranger.

She said, to change the subject, 'Have you seen the exhibition in the other room?'

One of the reasons for the party was to launch an exhibition of American-owned folk art. Katya had already been conducted round it by a seething Dmitri while he muttered of looters. The junior cultural attaché, to whom they were indebted for their invitation, had accompanied them and bore Dmitri's scowling restiveness with the blank charm of the professional diplomat. Katya had felt rather sorry for him, and dragged Dmitri away at the first possible moment in order to cut off his stream of complaint.

'Yes, I've seen it,' said Matt Saracen. 'And so have you. Who was the chap you were with?'

She was startled; she hadn't felt him looking at her in the gallery. It was only here, in the high-ceilinged reception room, that she had felt herself under scrutiny. She gave a little involuntary shiver.

However, she answered with outward composure, 'Dmitri Kolkanin. He's the director of the folk dance troupe.'

His eyes flashed down her body in one comprehensive glance. Katya, to her astonishment, found it left her feeling as if she had been sprayed with ice and stripped. It was oddly insulting, in spite of his lazy smile of approval.

'Hence the costume?'

'I'm a member of the group, yes,' she said stiffly.

'The star, no doubt.' He was smooth, but there was an edge to the remark.

'No. The most junior recruit.' Katya gave her low, warm laugh at the thought of Dmitri's horror if she had proposed herself for a solo. 'And I'm only allowed in on a special dispensation because one of the regulars has a job in Monte Carlo. Normally I just go to Dmitri's classes.'

There was an arrested expression on his face.

'Classes?'

'Thursday evenings,' she explained. 'It gives me a chance to keep up my Russian and take some exercise at the same time.'

There was a long pause and then, suddenly, he flung back his head and gave a great shout of laughter. It was a full-throated sound and many people turned their heads, smiling, to see who it was who was enjoying himself so much.

'Oh, honey, you must be the despair of Prince Casimir: "it gives you some exercise"! *Not* a sentimental gesture to Mother Russia, *not* a clinging to the old ways. And you're not even the star.'

Katya sniffed. It was a shrewd enough remark about her grandfather, but she didn't relish the way it reflected on herself.

'I like dancing,' she said in a remote voice, 'that's all.'

'And if the Russian stuff was on an inconvenient night, you'd do flamenco instead,' Matt commented, his eyes brimming with laughter. 'Wouldn't you?'

'I—well—yes, I suppose so,' she acknowledged.

'Princess, no wonder Prince Casimir blames your English grandmother. He can't have had a steady, sensible lady like yourself in his family for a couple of centuries. Allow me to congratulate you.' He made a little bow. 'You are a rare creature.'

Katya considered him, the wide eyes doubtful and a touch apprehensive.

'I think you know my family a good deal better than you led me to believe,' she said at last, slowly.

But he was not to be lured into telling her more.

'No,' he said decisively, shaking his head. 'No I don't know them at all these days. It was different ten years ago. But—things change—and I thought I would never meet or want to know another Andreyev in my life.' His eyes narrowed now and he was looking straight at her, into her she felt, and her whole body seemed to quiver with the intensity of it. 'I may be a fool,' he added softly, 'but I think I just changed my mind.'

CHAPTER TWO

AT work the next day, Katya turned that remark over and over in her mind. She had had no chance to ask him what he meant because immediately afterwards Dmitri had descended and bore her off to dance. When the dancing was over Katya had seen Matt in the distance but had no chance to talk to him. And then Dmitri had insisted on seeing her home.

She sighed. It had been long before the end of the party; nobody else was leaving, and Dmitri had been in one of his most dictatorial moods. He had talked to her as if she was four instead of twenty-four. Katya had told him so, and he had left her at her door in high offence.

Katya bit her lip, peering at the thermometer in the gas-chamber in front of her and making a careful mark on a piece of graph paper beside it.

'What is it?' her friend Babette Leon asked from her bench at the other end of the laboratory. 'Is there a leak?'

'What?' Surprised out of her reverie, Katya jumped, then she gave herself a little shake and turned to face the other girl. 'No, nothing like that. The reaction is proceeding beautifully, as far as I can judge.'

Babette wrinkled her small nose. 'Then why the worry, the knitted brow, the heavy sighs?'

Katya was startled. 'That bad?'

'If not worse,' nodded Babette, twinkling. 'It is not like you, either.'

There was a faint interrogative note in her voice, but Katya knew that Babette would not pursue the subject any further. They were very good friends, Babette recognised and respected Katya's need for privacy; she wouldn't intrude where Katya indicated that she didn't want her to do so.

Katya smiled at her gratefully, and sat down on one of the ancient splintery stools that had been in the laboratory since it was first set up in the 'twenties.

'It's Dmitri,' she confessed. 'I think I must have given him the wrong idea somehow—he's becoming very possessive.'

Babette looked intrigued. She knew Dmitri. Katya had introduced them and Babette had decided at the first meeting that, though she did not know Dmitri well enough to guess what he felt for Katya, she was sure that her friend did not and would never regard him as anything other than a friend.

'How does this possessiveness manifest itself?' she asked, abandoning all pretence at work and laying her pencil down on the bench.

Katya's face darkened. 'He had the gall to tell me off!'

'Tell you off?' echoed Babette in bewilderment. 'But for what?'

'For nothing,' Katya said heatedly. 'For talking to some man at a party. Which was none of his business.'

Babette's lashes veiled her eyes, and she made sympathetic noises.

'Well, tell me what you think,' Katya said. 'It was the American Embassy reception last night. We were dancing. Before the performance I met a man. . . .'

'Ah!'

'What do you mean, ah?' demanded Katya, put out.

Babette shrugged. 'But it is obvious, you silly girl. You meet a man who attracts you and Dmitri is displaced. Of course he is annoyed! And so he remonstrates.'

'I didn't say the man attracted me,' pointed out Katya.

Babette's eyes were shrewd. 'Doesn't he?'

'I——' Katya stopped, biting her lip.

'Dmitri obviously thinks he does,' pursued Babette.

The wide violet eyes were troubled. 'Yes, you must be right. He gave me a terrible lecture last night on innocent young women and the seducers of the world.'

'Good gracious,' said Babette, diverted, 'how very unsubtle, and not at all likely to put you off the man, either. What is he like?'

'Matt?' Unconsciously Katya's voice softened. 'Rather alarming, really. Sort of unpredictable. I think he may be very sophisticated.'

Babette was startled and even slightly concerned at this description, delivered in an uncharacteristically dreamy tone. But she only said, 'What does he look like?'

Katya considered the matter. 'He's very tall. You have to look up to him. That could be why he's so intimidating at first sight, I suppose. And elegant, though not in the French style.'

'Isn't he French?'

'No, American. I gather that was one of the things Dmitri objected to.'

'So what is he doing in Paris? Is he one of the Embassy diplomats?' asked Babette patiently.

'No, he's a pianist. Rather a famous one,' Katya added with reluctance.

Babette was amused. 'Poor old Dmitri! He's got himself the sort of rival that he will imagine you won't be able to resist.' Babette had discovered Dmitri's exaggerated respect for the rich and famous the first time she met him.

Katya gave a wry smile. 'I don't know about that. To judge by what he was saying last night, Dmitri think he's the devil incarnate.'

'*Quite* irresistible,' Babette assured her. 'Every woman is fascinated by a devil. And don't tell me you're any different, because I won't believe you.'

'Probably I'm not,' agreed Katya, sighing faintly, 'but don't get the wrong idea, Babette. It was a very ordinary conversation. He didn't try to chat me up or anything. There wasn't the slightest reason for Dmitri's behaviour, even if he had the right to be jealous of me, which he hasn't. No, Matt Saracen isn't the problem—it's Dmitri and this idea he has that he can run my life for me that bothers me. I'm going to have to tell him to back off, and I'm not looking forward to it.'

She said no more, but Dmitri rang twice during the day and on each occasion her expression, Babette noted, became more sombre. On a third occasion, just before they were due to leave work, she told the switchboard to say she had gone and, rising quietly collected her coat and left.

In her apartment block the concièrge, a deaf and garrulous lady, fell upon her with an excited tale of how Katya's young man had come to tell her all about last night's party. He was so nice and such a handsome man, he made her feel quite girlish. And he agreed with her that Mademoiselle André worked too hard, so he had come to make sure that tonight she did not work but enjoyed herself. She hesitated, a slight worry seeming to touch her for the first time. 'I'm sure I hope I did right, *mademoiselle*.'

'What did you do, *madame*?' asked Katya gently.

'Well, I let him in, like he asked me to. Into your room, *mademoiselle*.'

Katya's brows twitched together. Dmitri, she thought with a resurgence of fury, had a cheek! How dared he come round here and sweet-talk the poor old concièrge into letting him into her room, when he knew quite well that she didn't want to see him.

However, all she said to the anxious old face was, 'I'm sure it does not matter, *madame*. If I know him it will be all right. And if I don't,' she shrugged, 'well, there's nothing there of value for a burglar to steal. Don't disturb yourself. I'll just go and see what he wants.'

Forgetting her weariness, she ran up the stairs, simmering. At her door she could hardly get the key into the lock, she was shaking so much with rage. As she banged the door back on to its hinges she surged into the room in a flame of fury.

'How dare you come here like this? How dare you hound me? What the devil do you think you're doing, conning that poor old woman downstairs into letting you into my apartment? Don't you know she could lose her job for that if anyone got to hear of it?'

The man in her old swivel chair, who had been regarding the view from the window, swung himself round to look at her with her hair flying and eyes glittering with temper, and gave a soft laugh.

'And I thought you would congratulate me on my enterprise,' said Matt Saracen mournfully.

Katya felt as if all the breath had been literally punched out of her.

'*You!*'

His eyes narrowed watchfully, but he smiled.

'Whom were you expecting?'

She closed the door behind her very carefully, inspecting him. He looked very much at home, his long body lounging in the old chair as if it were an accustomed favourite, one hand resting along its arm.

'Not you, certainly,' she said in a cool voice, deliberately keeping all expression at bay.

Matt looked amused. 'Evidently.'

'My question remains the same, though,' Katya went on. 'What are you doing here?'

He stretched lazily, a movement which sent the muscles rippling under his open shirt. Katya registered it with a little shock; it must have shown on her face, because his smile grew.

'I wanted to see you.'

Katya sat down, smoothing her dark skirt over her knees with fingers that were not entirely steady.

'I am, of course, flattered,' she said politely. 'Though would it not have been easier to telephone than to—invade?'

'Invade?' His eyebrows went up and he was laughing. 'Now there's a dramatic word for you. And I was just thinking that you were a very cool lady who didn't go in for dramatics.'

'I don't,' Katya snapped crossly, feeling her cheeks grow warm. 'Why didn't you telephone?'

Matt laughed, looking eloquently round the room.

'How was I to do that? You have no phone of your own and I had the greatest difficulty in making your concièrge understand everything. I couldn't have trusted her with a message.'

'She's deaf,' conceded Katya with reluctance, 'but you could have rung me at work.'

He pretended to look shocked. 'And disturb you during your researches? Are you saying that you're permitted to make private telephone calls at your place of employment? Surely you don't approve of that?'

She said sweetly, 'I don't care for it, I admit, but I prefer it to being burgled.'

He gave that low, pleased laugh that she was coming to know.

'You're magic,' he said with apparent irrelevance, and swung himself to his feet. 'And you haven't been burgled. Yet.'

Katya didn't move as he strolled over to her; she had some idea that he was trying to intimidate her with his height and with the undeniable strength of the lean body. She tilted her head defiantly, looking up at him.

He came to stand in front of her chair, hands in the pockets of his jeans. 'Burglary,' he murmured in a reflective voice, 'involves theft. Positively demands it.' The eyes glinted wickedly, but his mouth was solemn and his voice even. 'And theft is the taking by force of that which is not given freely.'

In one fluid movement he was crouching beside her chair, laughing at her, eyes on a level with her own. He leaned forward.

'And you don't look as if you're in the business of giving freely,' he concluded calmly.

And reached for her.

Katya sat as if turned to stone, prey to too many emotions to pluck one out from the throng. She was outraged; she was faintly alarmed; she was even reluctantly amused. And she was too bewildered to make her escape before the firm mouth closed on her own.

It was a very gentle kiss; more of a question than the taking by force that he had threatened, Katya thought in surprise. Yet for all his gentleness she was quite sure that he would not brook resistance, were she to offer any. So she sat as still as a mouse while he brushed his lips lingeringly across her own, parting them, touching his tongue delicately to the softness within.

At length he loosed her, sitting back on his heels looking wry.

'There you are,' he said. 'Consider yourself burgled.'

'I do,' Katya told him in a distant voice. She was very proud of the fact that it didn't waver. The caress had shaken her, and her own instinctive response to it even more. She had suppressed it with apparent success, from his expression, but she could not disguise from herself the fact that his touch had moved her more than anyone else's had done before. She drew back a little. 'Is that what you came for, then?'

He shook his head. 'Hardly.'

'Then what?'

Matt seemed to hesitate: Katya had the impression that he was not just choosing his words but his whole approach with great care. She had an obscure suspicion that she was being manoeuvred in a battlefield that was wider than she was aware of. But even as her brows twitched together at the thought, he had stood up and was wandering round the room, hands in his pockets, like any other casual visitor.

'I wondered if you'd like supper,' he offered coolly over his shoulder.

'Supper?'

'Yes. Food. The evening meal. Sustenance. Or do you live on air and music, like princesses out of fairy tales?'

Katya smiled. 'I'm only a shadow princess, I'm afraid. And I eat like a horse.'

'I'm glad to hear it,' he said gravely. 'Let's share a trough this evening.'

She was tempted—he was too attractive for her not to be tempted. And he was amusing and stimulating and he made her feel alive. In ordinary circumstances she would have gone like a shot.

But the circumstances weren't ordinary. For one thing she really did not like him invading her room like that. For another, well, it was easy to say that Dmitri was an old woman and dismiss his catalogue of ancient scandal; but that wouldn't dismiss her own faint uneasiness about the man. For all his abundant charm, Matt Saracen was a stranger and, for a stranger, he was moving very fast towards an intimacy that Katya was by no means sure she wanted. And in those circumstances, a simple invitation to dinner became invested with other qualities, none the less alarming for being vague.

Sensing her hesitation, he said plaintively, 'I'm starving, and I have no idea where to get a reasonable meal in Paris.'

Katya was incredulous and said so.

'No, really! I've read all the restaurant guides and I haven't a clue. I don't want to eat so much that I can't move, and I don't want to pay so much that I have to starve for the next fortnight.'

'Couldn't you have asked your agent?' Katya asked, remembering that Matt had referred to this personage last night.

He grimaced. 'My agent thinks that what I need is a happy family dinner every night to make me feel secure and protected. What *that* means is that I have to drive miles out to the middle of nowhere, watch television, get climbed on by some of the stickiest children it has ever been my misfortune to meet, and eat at midnight. I then get lost in the *péripherique* coming back into town and spend the rest of the night suffering from indigestion.'

'Oh,' said Katya, wavering. 'It sounds horrible,' she allowed fair-mindedly.

Matt gave her his lop-sided smile.

'It *is* horrible, especially when there are better things to keep me awake than indigestion.'

He touched the back of his hand to her cheek as he spoke. She put up her own and brushed it away with great calm.

'There is not,' she said carefully, 'anything else to keep you awake in my company.'

The long mouth quirked.

'You underrate yourself.'

Katya shook her head.

'Believe me, I don't. If you want anything else,' she met his eyes with a half-smile, 'then you should look for another companion.'

His own eyes were unreadable as they locked with hers. She had the feeling, though, that behind the inscrutable expression he was weighing and evaluating what she'd just said and adjusting his tactics to deal with it. She felt a little *frisson* of alarm. What is it he wants of me? she thought suddenly; I'll swear he wants something.

Then he gave a shrug.

'Fair enough, you've made your point. If I promise to keep to my own side of the table and my hands on the cutlery, will you take pity on me?'

Katya laughed. 'If you give me time to change.'

He looked faintly alarmed. 'Do you want to go

somewhere grand?'

She shook her head. 'No, but I don't want to go anywhere in a blouse and skirt that smells of chemicals.'

He gave a theatrical sigh. 'That's a relief! I thought you were going to make me go back and climb into a dinner-jacket.'

Katya was standing up, making for her room, but at this she glanced at him curiously.

'Would it have mattered if I had?'

Matt laughed easily. 'Only in that I'm hungry and I don't want to waste any more time.'

'I see. I'll shower in thirty seconds, then,' Katya promised him lightly.

The reply had given her pause, though, and she did not entirely believe him. He might very well be hungry, he had probably been waiting for her some while. Yet it was not hunger that made him want to go somewhere informal, she was fairly sure, any more than it was economy. He hadn't looked exactly impoverished last night. It was—it had to be—that he did not want to go anywhere fashionable, where he might be seen with her. It was all right to flirt a little with an obscure graduate student when he was playing in a foreign city. It wouldn't do his image any good, though, if that unimportant flirtation made it into the newspapers along with all his previous escapades.

Well, Katya thought tolerantly, climbing into cotton pedal-pushers and a matching top, she would not embarrass him by demanding luxury restaurants and fashionable company. But equally she was not going to provide him with the casual sexual companionship that he was clearly used to finding available. She knew what that sort of affair could do to a girl: had she not Vonnie's experience as a bitter warning?

No, Katya had always steered well clear of involvement, both commitment and the sort of thoughtless occasional pact that Matt Saracen had in mind for tonight. She wasn't about to change. And if Matt Saracen did not believe her now, he would do so by the end of the evening.

CHAPTER THREE

THEY went to a small restaurant that Katya knew. It was simple but the cooking was good and it was, at least by Parisian standards, cheap. Mostly it was patronised by students and junior teaching staff from the university.

When they arrived the patron greeted Katya warmly; there was a welcoming nod of his head for Matt whom he plainly did not recognise. As they made their way to the table he indicated, one or two of the diners looked up to acknowledge Katya.

As they seated themselves at the scrubbed wooden table Matt said in amusement, 'You obviously come here often.'

Katya smiled. 'Whenever I can't face another cheese sandwich.'

Matt looked startled. 'Is that what you live on, then? Cheese sandwiches?'

She nodded.

'No wonder you look so ethereal,' he told her. 'You must be half-starved.'

'Cheese sandwiches are very nutritious,' she assured him. '*And* cheap. *And* easy.'

His eyes glinted with laughter. 'Not a gourmet, obviously.'

'I haven't the time or the money to be a gourmet,' she informed him. 'Cheese sandwiches are par for the course when you're a graduate student.'

He patted her hand sympathetically. 'It's what they call the intellectual pleasures, honey. I've done it myself and I remember.'

Of course, he had said he was at Oxford with Paul. Katya looked at him consideringly. He hadn't sounded as if he had particularly enjoyed his time there, either. She said, 'You sound as if you don't think it's worth it?'

Matt was studying the blackboard on which was written the day's menu. He brought his gaze back to her. 'What? The iron rations or the intellectual feast?'

'Both.'

He gave her a lazy smile. 'Then I belie myself. I'm sure it's worth it. If for nothing else because it teaches you to appreciate the good things of life.'

Katya was oddly disappointed. 'Things like gourmet meals?'

'You sound disapproving. Yes, good food among other things.'

The waiter arrived to take their order and Matt bent all his attention on it, making sure that Katya ordered a substantial dish. She shrugged impatiently, allowing him to choose whatever he wanted for her. When he had gone, she leaned forward urgently.

'You don't really mean that. You can't.'

Matt looked amused. 'Oh, I'm a great consumer. I like good wine and luxury apartments, fast cars and not too much work. I've never denied it, and the world's press has made sure everyone knows it. You'll have a tough job turning me into an idealist, Princess.'

She said slowly, 'Then how can you live by music?'

He shrugged. 'Playing the piano is a living like any other. You need a dash of talent, a dash of application and a hell of a lot of luck. I've had all three.'

There it was again, that slight bitterness that Katya had caught before.

Greatly daring, she asked, 'Are you happy with it?'

Matt shifted in his chair, looking round. 'The waiter is a long time bringing us that wine.'

But, 'Are you happy?' Katya persisted, sure, somehow, that this was important.

He lifted one shoulder. 'What's happy? I have

money in the bank and a lifestyle that's envied by millions.'

'And that's all that playing the piano is to you? A job, like bricklaying?'

He smiled suddenly, a real rueful smile. 'I guess I'd be happier as a bricklayer. At least then I'd be able to leave my job behind me at the end of the day.'

And then the waiter arrived with the unlabelled green bottle in which they served their *vin ordinaire* and it became impossible to continue the conversation. When he left, Matt turned the subject firmly: they were to talk about Katya, plainly.

She acquiesced, telling him about her studies, the other people in the laboratory, half of them technicians, half research workers like herself. She told him about her tutoring and some of her pupils' resistance to work. She even told him a little about her life in England before she had got her place at the French university.

'You sound very solitary,' he commented.

'Do I?' Katya was faintly surprised.

'You're never lonely?'

'No.' She was affronted at the idea.

'I find that odd.'

'I don't see why,' she said, bristling.

The grey eyes were hooded. 'And that's the oddest thing of all,' Matt said maddeningly.

'What is?'

'That you're a beautiful girl—free, intelligent, independent—and you divide your time between the laboratory and the classroom, with a touch of late-night reading for your thesis thrown in as light relief. And you seem to have no idea that your life is arid, or to resent it in any way. Still less,' he added in a brooding tone, 'are you willing to change it.'

She said defiantly. 'My life is what I choose.'

'I know.' He shook his head. 'It's tragic.'

She threw down her fork. 'Look, I didn't come out

with you so you could read me a lecture on the way I live!'

Matt's eyebrows, startlingly dark in spite of the copper hair, flew up.

'That sounds as if it's happened before.'

Katya smiled reluctantly. 'You're too quick,' she complained.

He was thoughtful, 'So I'm not the only one who thinks it is a rotten waste.'

'I didn't say that.'

Matt was amused. 'You didn't have to. You fly on to the defensive too quickly. It gives you away.'

Katya bit her lip.

'So what happened?' he asked gently. 'You went off people in your teens? You're allergic to men? You're on the run from the police?'

She gave a little choke of laughter at that last, solemnly delivered suggestion. Then she sighed.

'Perhaps it would be true to say I'm on the run, though not from the police,' she added wryly.

Matt took a slice of bread from the basket on the table and began to shred it away from the crust, crumbling the white stuff into a thousand pieces. He stared at the work in apparent absorption.

'So who?' he asked at last. And when she didn't reply, prompted, 'An old boyfriend? A discarded lover? A husband?'

Katya stared at the downbent head. For some reason which she couldn't explain she had the feeling that these questions were not nearly as teasing as the earlier ones. He did not suspect her of having a police record but he did, quite seriously, think she might have a trail of ruinous relationships in her wake. With her record of personal involvement it was almost funny, though Katya didn't feel like laughing.

She said shortly, 'You've got the wrong princess. You must be thinking of my cousin.'

His eyes rose, and he gave her a level look in which

she thought she read a good deal of comprehension. But all he said was, 'So, no jettisoned men. What about unrequited love?'

Katya gave a crack of laughter. 'I've never been in love, as they call it. I don't think I qualify. I'm too practical,' she expanded after a moment. 'At least that's what my grandfather used to say.'

Still that unwavering gaze and silence. Katya took a nervous sip of wine and looked away.

'I don't know what the phrase means, anyway,' she ended defiantly.

There was a pause and then Matt said slowly, almost as if he were talking to himself rather than to her, 'So what happens to the men who fall in love with you?'

She was startled. 'They don't.'

'Don't they? Are you sure?' The long mouth twisted. 'Or do you just not notice?'

Katya shook her head positively. 'Absolutely not.' It was her turn to be wry. 'Don't forget I've had a ringside seat for my cousin Vonnie's love affairs, of which I imagine you've heard, and I know the symptoms even if I don't understand the disease. Nobody has ever behaved to me like that.'

Matt stared at her, his eyes narrowing. 'And you're glad,' he said on a note of discovery.

Katya shivered suddenly. She recalled the frantic tears, the fights, the impassioned reconciliations and then the despair when yet another of Vonnie's undying relationships fell apart. It had been exhausting to watch: she was sure she couldn't live through even one such storm if she were in the centre of it.

She said, 'Who wouldn't be?'

'Most women . . . no, most people,' Matt corrected himself, 'want to feel themselves loved,' he ended on a faint query.

Katya shook her head with decision. 'Not me. I told you, I don't know what it means.'

'To be the centre of somebody's world,' Matt told

her softly. 'To share. To talk without words and understand without thinking. To care more for the beloved's pleasure than one's own. To laugh together. And to touch the stars.'

Katya caught her breath. There was no irony in his voice; he was not teasing her. He was not mocking. The calm voice could have been stating the components of one of her workday formulae. Yet for all his lack of intensity, Katya felt as if, without her noticing it, a high wind had blown up behind her and she was being borne along on it, too far and too fast towards the precipice.

She said, more harshly than she had intended to, 'That's romantic nonsense.'

'Is it?'

'Yes, and I'm surprised at you. I didn't think international sophisticates spent their time looking for love, true love,' she said with disdain.

Matt was unoffended. He even looked amused. 'Even international sophisticates can hope.'

She shrugged, not answering.

'Which is why I find it surprising that a beautiful young woman, with much more chance of finding,' his voice deepended echoing her words ironically, 'love, true love, than an old cynic like myself, should be so determined that it doesn't exist. And you *are*, aren't you? I've never seen a less open mind.'

Katya said, 'I may not know what it feels like, but I sure as hell know what it costs.'

There was a long silence. Behind them the restaurant buzzed with talk and the clatter of plates and glasses. It hardly reached them. They sat in a capsule of silence, their eyes locked. Katya felt as if she had been challenged, as if he were daring her to defend her views, though he said nothing. There was just the devastating silence and the unreadable grey eyes. Katya lifted her chin.

Matt said, 'The price is always high for something of value.'

Katya met his eyes squarely. 'And sometimes the price is higher than you can afford.'

'Even when it's worth it?'

'But you can't know whether it's worth it until afterwards. At the time, it's a gamble.'

He leaned forward. 'So is the whole of life.'

Katya shook her head, the dark hair swinging against her neck. 'Not my life,' she said firmly.

'Oh yes.' He was tranquil but very, very assured. 'Even yours. In spite of your protective routine and your cold little heart.' He gave her a lop-sided smile. 'As you'll find out.'

Dear God, thought Katya, drawing back in her chair as the waiter placed a plate in front of her, *it sounds like a threat*.

She picked up her fork and said in a neutral voice, 'How long are you going to be in Paris?'

Matt laughed softly. 'Time for a change of pace?' he asked and then, before she could say anything, answered her question. 'Another five days.'

Katya nodded, slightly surprised at the pang of disappointment she felt. She had always known that he was only a visitor, just passing through the city briefly. But it struck a blow, almost as if he were a long-established neighbour who had announced his intention of leaving. She frowned at her own lack of logic and asked briefly, 'Five days for one concert?'

'Would that it were.' Matt shook his head. 'I was recording last week, I have the first concert tomorrow and then another one the day after. And I'm giving a lecture and guesting on a chat show, and there are press interviews and we have to talk about my next concert series . . .' He looked wry. 'Five more full days, believe me. I still have to find time to practise, too.'

She was intrigued. 'Do you practise a lot? Do you have to?'

The thin clever face looked suddenly drawn. 'I can't answer that. I don't know. I never feel that I practise enough. But there's a school of thought which holds that I practise too much, and that's why . . .'

He broke off sharply, almost as if he had burned himself, and gasped at the unexpected pain.

After a pause, Katya prompted softly, 'Why . . .?'

Matt hesitated. Then he shrugged. 'Well, why not admit it? Why I'm not playing as well as I used to. Why the critics—or at least, the perceptive ones—are always saying these days that I haven't fulfilled my earlier promise.' His voice was light, hard. He sounded quite unmoved, and yet Katya was certain that beneath the cool exterior there was distress. She did not know how she knew it, for there was no outward sign, but she felt quite sure she was right.

She took a mouthful of food, thinking. Then she said, 'Are they right?'

'Oh yes,' said Matt dispassionately. 'They've been right for a long time. Fortunately,' he added with irony, 'it doesn't affect ticket sales. They come to see me not listen to the music, these international audiences. And I'm still the same: still drinking, still raising Cain, still having rows with conductors. I can guarantee to carry on delivering *that*, at least.'

Katya winced at the pain she could feel in him. 'You sound as if you hate your audience.'

Matt gave her a sudden smile; it changed his whole appearance, making him look younger and far less remote. 'Sometimes I do,' he admitted. 'It terrifies my agent.'

'I can understand that,' Katya said, allowing her amusement to show and keeping her real sympathy well hidden. 'I know you throw things at conductors you don't like. Do you do the same for audiences?'

'Not yet, though I've been tempted.'

'It seems very ungrateful to me,' she remarked, 'especially if they keep coming to see you whether you play well or not.'

He wasn't offended. His eyes narrowed, laughing. 'Yes, it does, doesn't it?' he agreed affably. 'That's the temperamental artist for you.'

She lifted her eyes. 'Are you? Temperamental, I mean? You don't sound it.'

'Don't I?' Matt was rueful. 'You should talk to my agent. He thinks I've got more temperament than anyone who isn't a genius is entitled to.'

'And have you?'

He looked at her. 'I don't know,' he said slowly, 'I honestly don't know. Sometimes I think I have nothing more than sufficient manual dexterity and a good memory. And sometimes . . .' He shrugged. 'I can't tell you. You'll have to make up your own mind.' He flashed her a quick look, unexpectedly serious. 'Come to my concert tomorrow night.'

Katya was shaken. It seemed to her that he was asking her for something that she didn't have the resources to give. She said hesitantly, 'I don't know very much about music.'

He grinned wryly. 'The way I'm playing at the moment, so much the better. Will you come?'

She said, 'I'd like to.'

'Good. I'll leave a couple of seats for you at the box office,' he said, and changed the subject.

She went to the concert alone. She had briefly contemplated asking Babette whether she would like to accompany her but decided against it. Babette was not particularly musical, and she would be bound to demand an explanation of where Katya had got her tickets and why. Dmitri, who was musical, was not of course a candidate. So the second ticket stayed unused, and she propped her shoulder bag on the empty seat beside her.

It must, she thought, faintly conscience-stricken, be the only empty seat in the house. The place was packed, and Matt was rapturously received. Watching him from her safe obscurity in the audience, Katya felt very strange. In his tails and frilled white shirt he looked remote and unfamiliar. And yet ... and yet ...

Slightly to her dismay, Katya felt as if she had known him all her life, almost as if she had a proprietorial interest in his elegant figure. She felt a surge of pride and affection when he made his entrance. She ached with nerves when he seated himself at the gleaming grand piano, and when he finished his first sonata, she felt limp with relief as he bowed to the crowd, receiving their acclamation with an unmoved expression.

What's happening to me? she thought, bewildered. How can I feel this close to a man I've only met twice? She discovered—and was horrified by—a strong inclination to go to him, to take the thin arrogant face between her hands and kiss away the look of tension. She pressed her hand against her hot cheek, blushing unseen as the house-lights went down for the start of the second part of the concert. How could she feel like this? Had she no self-control? No pride? He had barely kissed her, and here she was dreaming of throwing herself into Matt Saracen's arms.

She left as soon as the concert was over, pushing her way through the crowd, eager to get away before the unwelcome feelings could have their way and take her round to the stage door to see him. That embarrassment at least, she told herself grimly, she would spare them both.

The next morning she was sitting at her desk, drawing a careful graph, when the telephone at the far end of the laboratory rang. Henri Bauer, the Frenchman with whom she shared the laboratory routine, went to answer it. Then he called her name on a surprised note.

'For you, Katya. A Monsieur Saracen.'

She picked it up, saying in a puzzled voice, 'Catherine André.'

'It's me,' said the slightly drawling voice which set her pulses tingling.

'Oh,' she said rather helplessly. She felt her colour rise, and sensed rather than saw Henri's amusement as he moved tactfully to the other end of the room.

'You don't sound very pleased to hear from me. Was last night's playing so awful, then?'

'No. No, of course not,' Katya said in confusion, almost sure he was joking.

'You relieve my mind,' Matt teased. 'So when am I going to see you?'

'Oh!' Katya began to flounder. She hadn't got as far as imagining that they would meet again, at least not yet, not so soon. 'But you're busy. . . .'

'Not too busy to find time for important things. When?'

'I—I hadn't really thought about it.'

'Then think now,' he advised. 'What do you do in your lunch hour?'

'Walk round the park when it's fine enough,' she admitted honestly.

'It's fine enough. I'll meet you on the steps of the chemistry building at one,' he told her, and rang off.

She put the receiver down slowly, half amused and half vexed. She would have to tell Babette she could not meet her after all; the new shoes she was going to buy would have to wait until next week now.

When she heard the news, Babette's reaction surprised Katya. 'The rather famous pianist?' she asked. 'The one you were telling me about the day before yesterday? The one,' her voice grew heavy with irony, 'who didn't try to chat you up?'

'Yes,' Katya agreed, startled at the excellence of her friend's memory. 'How did you guess?'

Babette gave her a look of despair. 'He is the only

man you have ever talked about in two and a half years. It is not difficult to guess.'

'Oh.' Katya was slightly put out. 'Well, he telephoned and told me to meet him at one and then put the phone down before I could tell him that it wasn't convenient.'

Babette's eyes twinkled. 'Very wise,' she commented. 'He has taken your measure, by the sound of it.'

Katya was still brooding on that last enigmatic remark when she met Matt. He was waiting for her on the steps, as he promised, leaning up against a stone balustrade and surveying the people who passed him with an air of weary amusement. He was looking very tall and distinguished in a tweed jacket, fine shirt open at the neck, and cavalry twill trousers.

His eyes narrowed when he caught sight of her as she began to descend the steps. He straightened and came to meet her, taking both her hands between his long fingers; Katya looked down at their clasped hands, feeling suddenly shy. Matt did not attempt to kiss her.

'A punctual woman,' he said approvingly. 'I knew you were exceptional the first time I set eyes on you.'

She gave a nervous smile.

'And now we'll go and walk round that scrubby square which you mendaciously call a park and you'll tell me everything that's happened to you since we last met.'

Katya let him tuck her hand into the crook of his elbow, and fell into step beside him.

'But nothing *has* happened to me,' she protested. 'How could it? We last met only thirty-six hours ago.'

'Thirty-seven hours and four minutes,' he corrected. 'And plenty has happened. You came to my concert, though not backstage afterwards. Why?'

Katya walked beside him in silence for a little. She

didn't pretend to misunderstand him. At last she said, 'I didn't want to intrude. You would have all your friends there, and I'm not . . .'

'Not a friend?'

She shook her head. 'I didn't mean that, quite. But not one of the company of your friends.'

Matt said bleakly, 'You were wrong. I had no friends there. A few hangers-on, no more.'

Katya said, 'I'm sorry.'

'So am I. I was hoping . . .' He shrugged. 'Oh well, it's over, thank God.'

'Don't you like playing?'

He made a face. 'Not the way I played last night. Did you see the reviews?'

She shook her head.

'You haven't missed much. They are best described as mixed. Lots of bouquets for my flawless technique.' His mockery was savage.

Katya was bewildered. 'What's wrong with that?'

'Nothing. They're quite right—very fair indeed. The critics, at least the discerning critics, are saying that my playing is all fireworks and no feeling,' he told her. 'And they're not wrong. Old Albecin said my technique was "like sheet steel, shining, flawless, flexible and cold". Rather good, I thought. A memorable turn of phrase.'

Katya slid her hand down his arm to entwine his fingers. He stopped, looking down at her, and then, squeezing her hand, resumed their walk in silence.

Eventually Matt said in a different voice, 'I'm sorry, I didn't intend to take it out on you.'

She said calmly, 'It doesn't matter. But are things really so bad?'

He shrugged. 'What's bad? My career is going just fine. I'm making money hand over fist.'

'But you're not happy.'

'No,' he said, 'no, I'm not happy. And I don't know why.' They walked on in silence for a while and then he said in a reflective voice, 'Do you know that when I first saw you, when I talked to you, I had the feeling that you could tell me why? Isn't that the craziest thing you ever heard?'

CHAPTER FOUR

KATYA couldn't banish that remark of his from her mind. Though he had immediately turned the conversation into other, impersonal channels, it had come across with an intensity which left it echoing in her memory. Yet he had said nothing to reinforce it, nor had he made any further arrangement to meet her. And when she tentatively suggested that she might go to his next concert that night he had rejected the idea almost brusquely.

Three weeks later she was beginning to wonder whether she had imagined the whole thing. It was after the telephone in the laboratory had rung and Katya had leaped from her place looking strained, only to return with dragging steps when the call turned out to be for Henri, that Babette Leon took her to task.

'Look,' she said, placing a well-kept hand on Katya's graph paper so that she looked up, 'how much longer are you going to go like this? You're making me nervous.'

'Like what?' Katya hedged, tugging at her graph.

'Like a spider in overdrive,' said Babette crisply, 'a web a minute. It's exhausting to watch.'

'I enjoy my work,' Katya said defensively.

'Sure, so do I. But not at a hundred miles an hour.' Babette removed the whole block of graph paper and put it on the bench behind her. 'You're going to make yourself ill if you don't slow down. *And* stop jumping for the moon every time that telephone rings. Who is he?'

Katya folded her hands in her lap, since they had been deprived of her graph, and looked away.

'The pianist?'

If Babette had been simply inquisitive, if she had been censorious or amused, Katya would have told her to mind her own business. But her voice was so full of genuine concern that she couldn't.

'I—yes,' she admitted on a long sigh.

'So what happened?' Babette asked. 'A one-night stand and a long goodbye?'

It was an appalling thought. 'No,' said Katya, shuddering, 'not as bad as that.'

Babette's kind brown eyes clouded. 'There's no need to look so horrified, my dear. These things happen.'

'Not to me,' Katya said firmly. Then, seeing that Babette was in two minds about believing her, added with great earnestness, '*Really* not, honestly.' Her mouth twisted. 'He hardly even kissed me.'

'Sometimes that doesn't make a great deal of difference,' Babette told her, but she seemed relieved. 'So what is it that you are now running away from so hard? The fact that he didn't kiss you? Is this a bad case of unrequited love?'

Katya's eyes met hers in real puzzlement. 'I don't know, Babette. I don't understand him. Or myself, for that matter. One moment it seemed as if we were— well, together, I suppose. As if we weren't strangers. As if we knew each other's secrets and understood them. He felt it too, I know he did.'

Her voice trailed away as she looked back over those three crucial meetings. What was it that they'd said that made her feel they were so indissolubly bound together? And what on earth was it she'd done that had sent him away like that? Unless, of course, he had *not* felt it; she had been mistaken, and all he wanted was a brief, undemanding affair while he was in Paris and, discovering that he would not get it from her, had decided to cut his losses.

Babette looked at her with compassion. Her own husband flitted in and out of her life as his own needs dictated; she wasn't a stranger to the bewilderment that Katya was now suffering.

'But?' she asked gently.

Katya came back to the present. 'But the next moment he'd gone without a word.'

Babette inspected her fingernails, unable to watch the look of unhappiness in the expressive violet eyes.

'Do you know where he's gone? Have you tried to contact him?'

'How? I know he's left France, that's all. I don't even know whether he's still in Europe.'

'You could find out,' Babette pointed out gently. 'From whoever arranged his concerts here, for a start.'

'Yes, I've thought of that. But . . .'

Babette said nothing.

'How can I chase him?' burst out Katya. 'If he wants to see me again he knows where I am. If he doesn't get in touch, I have to assume that he's—regretting—knowing me before.'

'If you weren't lovers, I imagine that is more than possible,' Babette agreed drily. 'All the more reason for you to make the first move. He must have his pride too, after all.'

Katya shook her head decisively. 'I can't.'

'You'd rather be miserable? And jumpy? And lonely?'

Katya glared. 'If necessary, yes.'

Babette stood up. 'You're mad.'

Katya gave a deep sigh, looking down at her hands. 'Don't you see, Babette? If I get in touch with him it will mean that I've made up my mind, that I'm prepared to have an affair with him. And I'm still not sure that that's what I want, so I can't let him think it is.'

'You're living in the dark ages,' Babette informed her despairingly. 'Did he *ask* you to have an affair with him?'

'No, not exactly . . .'

'You say he didn't even kiss you?'

'Yes, but . . .'

'So what has the poor fellow done to have you handing him off as if he's some sort of latter-day Don Juan?'

There was no answer to that. Or rather there were two answers, and she could not tell Babette either of them. One was the undercurrent of sensual awareness that flowed between them all the time, that had been present even in that one gentle touch of the lips that she did not categorise as a real kiss. Her flesh held the memory of it still, though, and she was tremulous when she recalled it. The other, and by far the more frightening, was that he knew Vonnie, and hence knew what Andreyev ladies were capable of.

Katya reached for her workpad. 'It's no use, Babette. It's over—I'll get used to it. All the more quickly, if I'm allowed to work.'

Babette shrugged. 'Well, it's your life. And there's always a shoulder in rue Toulouse when you need it to cry on.' She touched Katya's shoulder briefly in sympathy, and strolled away.

The only other person to mention Matt to her was Dmitri. The Russian was openly jubilant that Matthew Saracen had left Paris, and he was inclined to be censorious.

'I warned you,' he said at the Russian Club in an intermission between dances. 'I told you what he was like, that he wanted you to be a passing intrigue, and you would not listen. You said it was my imagination. You said he did not want you. And now, look at you!'

'It's not very kind of you to crow, Dmitri,' Katya complained, trying to smile.

He was very pleased with himself. 'I say this only for your own good,' he said with patent untruth. 'You were lucky that he got bored so soon.'

Katya winced, but couldn't help laughing at Dmitri's monstrous insensitivity.

'I'm sure you're right,' she said, leaving him.

The next dance was beginning so he could not follow her, and at the end of the evening, when he was showing every sign of intending to walk home with her, she slipped away while he was talking to a new member. It was almost more than she could bear, to be reminded by Dmitri's heavy-handed censure that there had been a few brief hours when she and Matt Saracen had looked as if they might become lovers.

She was haunted by a sense of missed opportunity. It wasn't that she wished things had been different: she knew that. As she had told Matt, she had first-hand evidence of what these casual affairs could cost the participants and she didn't want to find herself in that position. Yet she could not shake off a feeling of regret.

Katya reproved herself for the feeling. It was idle, fanciful, a self-indulgence. She listed all its unacceptable qualities. It was juvenile, too. She was too mature to fall into a fit of romantic melancholy, she told herself fiercely. Yet it kept returning unbidden; that sense that she had closed a door that would never open again.

She did her best to banish it, staying long hours at the laboratory until Henri forcibly ejected her. Then she would walk home through the airless streets, trying to repress tantalising memories and equally tantalising speculation of what might have happened if . . . She invariably reached her flat out of breath and out of temper. She would then brew coffee and do her best to concentrate on her thesis.

It was on one such occasion, as she struggled with equations that would not add up, that a knock came at the door. It was so unexpected that she jumped, knocking over the mug at her elbow that was still half-full of cooling coffee.

'Damn!' she said, opening the door and flying immediately back to the table with a box of tissues. 'Come in,' she flung over her shoulder, mopping hard at the liquid that was seeping towards her papers.

'Thank you,' said an amused voice, the slight drawl much in evidence.

Katya stopped dead. The tissue in her hand grew sopping and she took it away mechanically, tossing it at the waste-paper basket. Then she turned.

Matt Saracen stood in the doorway, smiling at her. Katya opened her mouth to speak, found she had nothing to say and shut it again, feeling helpless. She put both hands behind her and braced herself against her desk. Her legs, she found, were trembling.

He looked at her quizzically, one dramatic black eyebrow raised. He looked cool and handsome and very relaxed. The Titian hair had been cut since they last met, she saw; otherwise he looked the same, from his arrogant profile to his whole challenging air. And the eyes, of course, were the same, intent and teasing and just a little shadowed, as if he knew a secret.

He still alarmed her.

Katya swallowed. 'H-hello.'

Matt strolled into the room and shut the door carefully. 'Hi. Having a small earthquake?' he asked, nodding at the upset mug.

Katya cast a look over her shoulder at the disarray on her desk. 'I overturned it when you knocked. I was startled, I don't get many visitors.'

'And when you do, you let them in without even finding out who they are?' Matt shook his head and the light gleamed on the flaming hair. 'Not very wise.'

Katya had to swallow again. Her mouth was very dry, and she ran her tongue over her lips. 'I suppose not.'

His eyes darkened. He walked towards her, his gaze never leaving her lips.

'Anybody could have been there,' he told her, in a caressing tone.

'Y-yes.'

'Anything might have happened.' He reached for her. 'And probably will,' he added mischievously before he kissed her.

It was as if she had been waiting for him for days, even years. She made not the smallest protest as her head tipped back and she was offering him her mouth. He kissed her thirstily, holding her so tight against his body that she could feel the imprint of the buttons on his shirt against her skin.

At length he lifted his head and looked down at her searchingly.

'Missed me?'

Katya nodded, a little shamefaced.

'Good.'

Another fierce kiss, his hands pressing hard in the small of her back while she strained against him, giving him kiss for kiss with a passion she had never dreamed she possessed. Her fears were swept away; all uncertainty disappeared. There was nothing left but the blinding need they felt for each other.

At last he put her away from him, holding her at arm's length, cradling her face between his hands. His breathing was not even ruffled, she noted, though his hands were not entirely steady.

'Missed me enough to go out with me this evening?' he asked softly.

Katya stared at him. 'What do you mean?'

His mouth twisted. 'You weren't exactly wild about the idea the last time we met.'

The violet eyes filled with genuine puzzlement. Had she not been wondering what it was she'd done to send him away like that? It hadn't occurred to her that Matt might think that she wanted him to go.

'Sweetheart, every word you said made it very plain you weren't interested in relationships in general and

Matt Saracen in particular,' he said, answering her unspoken question. 'When you didn't come backstage after my concert, well . . .' He shrugged. 'That just confirmed what I'd already guessed.'

'But it was you . . .' she gasped. 'After we met that lunch hour you never called me again or tried to see me. I thought you didn't want to.'

Matt gazed down into her eyes, frowning.

'Truly,' she emphasised.

'So you thought I'd lost interest,' Matt said slowly. His hands fell away, though he did not move back. 'What did you feel about that? Hurt? Surprised? Angry?' He gave a soft bitter laugh. 'Or nothing?'

'I—don't know.'

There was a long silence. She tried to meet his gaze frankly. At last he said, 'Well, that's honest, I suppose.'

'Matt—try to understand. I know it must be commonplace for you, but I'm not like that. I'm not impulsive. And what did we have?' She spread her hands. 'Five days while you were in Paris. I'm just not the type to build a relationship in five days.'

'If we'd had longer, would you have wanted to?'

But she just shook her head violently, the soft hair flowing about her shoulders and tangling in his fingers. Matt gave a long sigh.

'I suppose you don't know that, either.'

Katya said with difficulty, 'It's just that I don't do things like that. I know it's supposed to be a bad thing—and you'll probably laugh at me—but I'm the sort of person who doesn't enjoy new experiences. Particularly not when I know the dangers. And in your case the dangers have been very well charted,' she ended with irony.

Matt did not smile. 'You mean you ran away because of the damned scandal sheets?' He sounded incredulous.

'Partly.'

'And the other part?'

Katya met his eyes steadily. 'My natural wariness, vicarious experience, and an ingrained dislike of setting out on a road where I can't see the end.'

'Oh, Katya . . .' He pushed an impatient hand through his hair, looking disturbed. 'Nobody can ever see the end of any road. You have to gamble a little.' He stopped, then said, 'Start now: have dinner with me.'

She didn't answer at once, her indecision palpable.

He said very levelly, 'I shouldn't have come back to Paris, you know. It wasn't on my schedule.'

Surprised, she asked, 'Where should you be, then?'

He shrugged indifferently. 'New York, chained to my piano, writing a film score. It's been hanging round my neck for months, and if I don't put my mind to it now, I'm not going to get it finished. And I always deliver. It's what I'm noted for. I may not be a genius, but, by God, I'm professional.' He paused. She stared at him, a little afraid, though she did not know why. His voice gentled. 'Only I ran away this time. Nobody knows I'm here. Not my agent. Not my—family. Just you.'

The feeling of apprehension grew. Something large and jagged seemed to have stuck in her throat; when her voice came out, it rasped nervously.

'Why are you telling me this?'

Matt's look was ironical. 'That's the wrong question, Princess. You should be asking why I've come back.'

She flinched away from it, flinched physically as if from a blow. He noted the movement and his mouth tightened.

'No, you don't want to know that, do you?' He took her hands in a loose clasp, warm and infinitely reassuring. 'So I won't tell you. As for the rest——' again he lifted his shoulders, 'I suppose I was trying to point out that the gamble wouldn't be entirely one-sided. That I was risking something too.'

As if it was dredged up from the bottom of her deepest self, Katya said suddenly and harshly, 'I do *not* want to have an affair with you.'

The words hung between them, shocking in their stridency. Matt's grip tightened. Then, as if with a deliberate determination to reassure her, it relaxed again.

He said carefully, 'I am not—right at this moment—asking for an affair. I can't see that far down the road either.'

Torn between suspicion and hope, Katya searched his face for some clue to his real feelings. She found nothing to help her. He didn't look aggrieved or affronted or even very surprised; but then, if he was the practised seducer of women that Dmitri Kolkanin described, he would have learned not to react unguardedly. One thing she was sure of—Dmitri had been right when he said Matt Saracen wanted her. What he had left out—which she devoutly hoped he had not discovered—was that she, Katya André, cool, sensible and unimpassioned, wanted Matt Saracen with equal and possibly uncontrollable force.

She muttered, 'But it's what you normally expect.'

Matt laughed, not very humorously. 'Normal expectations aren't applicable with you, Princess. I've found that out, at least.' He gave her hands a little shake. 'Look, I accept that you don't want an affair, and I can handle that. But does that have to mean that you won't see me at all?' A coaxing tone, laced with laughter, entered his voice. 'You got away with your tail-feathers the last time we had a meal. Why not this evening?'

The attraction was powerful; Katya could not deny it. Something she didn't recognise was urging her to agree to whatever he asked. Imperceptibly her body moved, the resistance draining out of her; in another moment she would be swaying towards him. She shut her eyes, shuddering. Was this how Vonnie felt every time she announced that she was desperately in love? Was this the feeling that made her so icily selfish? Would it have the same effect on Katya herself?

Matt said softly in her ear, 'Are you going to run away from yourself for ever?'

Startled, she opened her eyes and looked at him. He was very close, too close. The grey eyes were slatey, unreadable, very bright like the Paris pavements after a shower of rain. Katya sensed his determination; it was, she thought wryly, the same implacable determination that Vonnie could show at times.

She said bitterly, 'I'm not your type, you know.'

He laughed. 'I don't know any such thing. Prove it.'

She smiled, but reluctantly. 'I'm not like my cousin. I don't know very much.'

Matt's eyes narrowed. 'Well, know this. If you were like your cousin I would still be in New York.'

Katya was taken aback, but he said no more and she forbore to question him. Surrendering to the inevitable, she bent her head until it rested against his shoulder.

'All right,' she said, 'dinner. Nothing else.'

'Noted.' He sounded amused, unconcerned. Was that because he didn't doubt his ability to persuade her into doing anything he set his mind to? Or because he genuinely didn't care? He gave her a little push. 'I'll wait while you climb into your glad rags.'

She shook her head, confused. Last time they had patronised a very ordinary little local restaurant.

'Are we going anywhere special, then?'

'Anywhere I can persuade you to accompany me is special,' Matt told her solemnly, his eyes dancing. 'And yes, this time we're going for flickering candlelight, sweet music and thousands of calories.'

Katya laughed but looked at her watch. 'Won't it be a bit early? This is Paris, you know. The serious eating doesn't start until the sun's gone down.'

'First,' he told her, 'we're going to have a drink in a bar that a friend of mine owns, and then we're going to wander hand in hand by the river. I intend to do this thing properly.'

She gave a slow, sweet utterly uncontrollable shiver at his words. A delicate flush rose under her skin, and Matt's eyes warmed. He took her hand and drew it gently across his parted lips.

'You will enjoy yourself,' he assured her softly, 'I promise.'

Katya knew he wasn't talking simply about a cocktail or a walk by the Seine, and her flush deepened. She withdrew her hand and said not very steadily, 'I—I'll go and change, then.'

And fled.

After that the evening went more or less as he had predicted. First of all they went to a basement bar that Katya, in spite of living a mere ten minutes' walk away from it, hadn't even known existed. It was cheerful and fairly full, in spite of the season. Most of the patrons, she discovered, were expatriate Americans. Several of them seemed to know Matt. She recognised the young diplomat who had organised the trade reception where she had danced; he looked at her curiously, but she did not think the recognition was mutual. He was more interested in Matt.

'Hi! Didn't expect to see you back in Paris, France until next year.'

Matt smiled. 'I don't tell the Embassy everything, Jack. This is a non-playing visit.'

'So the maestro gets a holiday?' The man's eyes slid round to Katya and he grinned. 'Well, congratulations.'

Matt's mouth tightened and the arm that was resting lightly round Katya's waist was suddenly as tense as steel.

'Not a holiday. I'm still working, just not in public.

Call it a private visit if you like. After all, who in his right mind stays in New York in August?'

'Sure, sure,' agreed Jack, still grinning. 'Well, we won't expect to see you in the Embassy, then.'

'Don't,' agreed Matt, beginning to turn away, but the friendly diplomat was not to be shaken off so easily.

'How's the work?'

'OK.' Katya could sense impatience and more than that in the reply. She looked up at him, frowning a little; was there really something wrong with his work that he wasn't admitting? And did she know him well enough to ask, or did he want to keep their relationship out of that area of his life? For that matter, did she want to get involved?

'And Steffy?'

Matt gave a laugh, relaxing. Whatever else he might mind talking about, Steffy Solomon was clearly not a sore subject, Katya noted.

'I haven't seen her since my concert here. I'm told she's shooting in the South of France.'

'Trust Steffy,' Jack agreed appreciatively. 'I bet she chooses her locations before she ever looks at the scripts. And Brett? How was he when you left?'

Matt stiffened again. His arm tightened round Katya so sharply that she had to suppress a gasp, but when he answered his voice was cool.

'Seemed fine when I saw him.'

'Still planning a new film?'

'Planning several, I believe.'

Jack shook his head. 'You've got to hand it them, that generation is wonderful. I only hope I have half his energy at his age.'

'He's always had plenty of energy,' Matt said in a colourless voice. He looked down at Katya. 'What will you drink, darling? Wine? A cocktail? What about one of those sky-blue jobs that Sim is making up now?' nodding to the bar.

Katya felt chilled. To be called *darling* in that light, sophisticated voice disconcerted her, and made her feel as if he could not remember her name. His eyes had a queer, blank look too; his mind was clearly elsewhere.

She said quietly, 'Sky-blue would be fine.'

The diplomat left them at last. Matt got the drinks and came back to her, but although he was polite, even affectionate still, he seemed to her to have withdrawn inside himself. She found herself chattering to fill the silence. It was only when the beautiful cocktail proved to taste of washing-up liquid that Matt roused himself and returned to the present to laugh at her expression.

After that the evening was back on track.

They walked under the long shadows by the river as the sun dipped to the horizon. There were other people about, tourists mainly, and plenty of stalls selling books and maps, or souvenirs or even flowers. Matt held her hand all the time and made her tell him about her life in Paris; it was companionable and unthreatening. Katya felt soothed and oddly comforted, as if Matt were promising to take care of her in this friendly stroll.

The restaurant, where he was clearly well known, was quite simply magnificent. It was famous; Katya recognised the name at once as soon as they arrived, although she had never been there nor knew anyone else who had. It was by far too expensive for her friends.

The discreet lighting, the attentive waiters were all that Matt could have wished. The soft piano that played in the background was cool and sweet without being intrusive, and the food, perfectly cooked and served with exquisite care, was an experience that she would never forget, Katya assured him.

He smiled. 'Good. I don't like to think of you forgetting anything you've done with me.'

Katya tensed but replied equably, 'Well, this is

certainly unforgettable! I've never had a meal like it. It's a whole new cultural experience.'

'And you enjoyed it?'

A smile curled her mouth. 'Who wouldn't?'

Matt reached out and took her hand. 'So we've demonstrated that you do sometimes enjoy new experiences?'

Katya swallowed, sitting ramrod-stiff.

'Haven't we?' he demanded, wicked laughter in the grey eyes.

She looked at him frostily. 'If that's the way you want to think of it.'

'Oh I do,' he assured her wryly, 'I need to. It's the only thing that gives me hope right at this moment.'

CHAPTER FIVE

HE had taken her home shortly after that disturbing exchange, and Katya had walked beside him almost silent. She was worried. It was so easy to enjoy his company, to relax under the sunny influence of his charm, to ignore the possible consequences. And then, just when she'd dropped her guard and was at peace with him, he would say something that reminded her of those consequences. He had never said he would be content with the simple friendship that was all Katya had to offer, and, brought back to awareness of the powerful attraction that hummed between them like taut wire, Katya could not convince herself that he would be content with it.

At her door, though, he made no attempt to touch her. Thanking her gravely for a delightful evening, he stood a decorous two paces away from her and maintained that distance throughout their brief farewells. Confused, Katya went to bed and, for the first time since leaving her grandparents' flat, found that she had too much on her mind to sleep.

What did he want from her? What, in the end, would she want to give him? Why did she think there was something he was not telling her, something important, when she had not the faintest reason for her suspicion? Why was she convinced that if she was not careful, he would hurt her mortally?

Yet when he telephoned her the next day she was overwhelmed with a rush of pleasure.

'I won't waste your time at work,' he told her in a brisk, unlover-like tone. 'I just wanted to make sure that I could see you tonight.'

Katya gave a little choke of laughter at this

peremptory invitation.

'What are you laughing at?' Matt demanded suspiciously.

'Your—er—style,' she informed him. 'You don't sound as if you have many doubts that you're going to see me tonight.'

'Then I sound stronger than I feel,' he said wryly. 'Are you turning me down, then?'

Katya hesitated. Oh, she wanted to see him! The telephone exuded an eloquent silence.

'Yes,' she said at last, slowly.

'Right,' he was brisk again. 'I'll pick you up at eight. There's an old movie I want to see. We'll go to that and I'll feed you afterwards.'

And he put the telephone down, leaving her no opportunity to protest.

As it turned out, she didn't want to protest. The film was exciting, one she had never heard of, and brilliantly acted. Afterwards they ate in a bistro at a table on the sidewalk, watching the world saunter past, and serenaded from time to time by a relaxed young man with a guitar. Katya sipped her wine, sighing with pleasure.

'You know,' she told him consideringly, 'you're very unexpected.'

'I am?' He had been looking at the guitarist and he swung round to face her, surprise evident on his face. 'In what way?'

She laughed, gesturing round the café.

'One night five-star de luxe, the next a humble student café.'

One eyebrow rose. 'You prefer luxury?'

Katya shook her head. 'It was fun—and very flattering to be taken there—but this is the sort of place at which I am at home. I'm not looking round all the time to see who's here and what they're eating. I know the menu and I've grown familiar with the wine, so I can concentrate on the conversation.'

Matt gave her a slow smile. 'You mean you weren't concentrating on *me* last night?' he teased.

She smiled back. 'Last night I was Cinderella at the ball. I was concentrating on the ball.'

He shook his head, mock-reproachful. 'If Cinderella thought like you, she'd never have got her handsome prince.'

Katya gave him a dry look. 'Quite.'

He laughed out loud at that, his hands reaching for hers across the iron table.

'You're shockingly unromantic. I shall have to take you in hand.' He paused thoughtfully. 'Perhaps a serenade at midnight beneath your window?' he mused, his eyes dancing.

'I'd be kicked out of the block,' Katya assured him. 'They're very insistent that tenants must be quiet.'

'Hmm. Well, I don't want to render you homeless,' he allowed. 'I shall have to think about it.'

'That sounds ominous,' Katya returned lightly, and began to talk about the film.

She didn't really think that he would embarrass her by singing beneath her window, as she remarked to Babette Leon at work the next day. Babette was more than a colleague, she was as close a friend as Katya had ever made. They'd even shared a flat for a while before Katya found her present apartment and Babette's husband, a footloose character who said marriage made him feel claustrophobic, had returned to the marital home. Since then Pierre had left Babette again, a subject on which Babette was uncommunicatively philosophical. He would, she said with resignation, return when it suited him.

In spite of the problems of her own marriage, Babette, who was a romantic, never ceased recommending the married state to Katya. At the news of this promising encounter, her eyes sparkled.

Katya said hastily, 'It was a joke. He wouldn't really do it.'

Babette looked sceptical. 'How can you be sure?'

'He's—well, he's too sophisticated.' Katya was confused. 'He wouldn't care to make a fool of himself.'

Babette gave a kindly laugh. 'You know far too little of men to make such sweeping assertions. He risked a pretty comprehensive snub by asking you out in the first place, didn't he?'

'That wasn't in public.'

'True, but you could have told people. No,' Babette shook her fair head in satisfaction, 'he doesn't sound to me to be the sort of man who bothers what other people think. If he wants to serenade you at midnight, he will.'

Katya lifted her chin defiantly. 'I may not know much about men, I can't deny that. But you don't know Matt at all.'

'I know the type, though,' Babette announced, suddenly sober. The look she gave Katya was very straight. 'They are very charming, these unconventional characters. They shake you up, open your eyes, cast a little spell. *But*——' she bit her lip, looking away, 'and it is a big *but*—they are like schoolboys: full of self-will, with never a thought for tomorrow.'

Katya flinched, as much from the distress in Babette's voice as from what she was saying about Matt. She knew very well that Babette was talking about Pierre. Matt, though she was still wary of him, was, she knew already in her bones, a different character from Babette's shallow husband.

So she said lightly, 'Now that's just where you're wrong. He never says good night without booking himself in for another excursion the next day. I sometimes wonder whether he thinks of anything else *except* tomorrow.'

Babette's eyes widened at this piece of information, but she said nothing more than, 'Interesting.' Then, with a look at her watch, 'I am sorry to be a bore, *chérie*, but I am due back to watch my cauldron bubbling in exactly four minutes. With so many people on holiday, there is only me and Dr Heinzel to keep the laboratory running.'

Katya acquiesced, standing up and stretching in the sunlight.

'Yes, I must get back too.'

Babette gave her an assessing look. 'You know, you could be devastating if you put your mind to it,' she announced.

'Thank you.' Katya was unmoved. They began to walk towards the chemistry building and she added, 'I don't see myself as a *femme fatale*, though.'

'No, I can see that,' Babette was thoughtful, 'and you don't even make the best of yourself. I find that very unusual. And I ask myself, why? Just as I ask myself, why no lovers?'

Katya gave her uninhibited laugh. 'Because I'm not a sophisticated Frenchwoman with the art of dressing in my genes,' she teased.

Babette smiled, plainly unconvinced. 'It is because of someone in the past?' she hazarded. 'An affair which went wrong, perhaps?'

Katya shook her head. 'Nope, no dramatic history. I've just never been interested.'

'That is what I find incredible. So young, so delightful and yet not to be interested in passion.' Babette shook her head. 'It is unbelievable.'

Katya thought of Vonnie, whose interests had been virtually confined to passion and romance for years, and gave a little shiver. But her smile stayed steady. Good friend though she was, Babette had not been told about the tensions of the Andreyev family.

'Still, it's the truth.' She shrugged. 'I'm a cold-hearted creature, Babette.'

But that her friend would not allow. She had been too understanding when Pierre Leon returned, offering immediately to vacate the small flat and give the couple much-needed privacy; too kind, also, after Pierre's eventual departure.

'You are a good friend,' Babette said soberly. 'But with men you are perhaps a little—how shall I put it—rigorous?'

Katya's eyebrows rose.

'You don't give them the benefit of the doubt,' Babette explained.

They had reached the building, and Katya inserted herself into the swing doors, glad that she did not have to answer. There was more than a grain of truth in the accusation.

She was reminded of it that evening as Matt took her hand while they were strolling along the Boulevard St Michel in the dusty twilight. It was an easy, casual gesture but at once Katya stiffened. His hold tightened and he glinted a look down at her.

'Relax, I'm only doing the proper thing,' he said in an amused tone.

Katya turned a blank face to him.

'Couples usually walk hand in hand,' he explained, a hint of exasperation feathering his tone.

Katya carefully left her hand limp and unresponsive. 'We're not a couple,' she observed dispassionately.

For a moment she thought she had angered him, then she saw that she had been deceived by the sparkle in the dark grey eyes. In reality he was laughing at her.

'No? We have a third companion?'

She shrugged, refusing to be drawn. 'You know what I mean.'

'Oh yes.' Suddenly Matt sounded tired. 'I know what you mean, Princess. And of course we do have a third companion: your suspicion.'

Katya was startled. 'I don't understand.'

'Don't you?' His look was enigmatic.

'No.' She moved her hand agitatedly in his, trying to free her fingers, but he wouldn't let her go.

'What if I tell you it's like going out with a CIA agent—you're always looking for signs of depravity in me. Sometimes I wonder if you've got a notebook where you write them down.' There was no mistaking the bitterness there.

'You're mistaken,' she stammered.

Matt denied it with a swift, decisive shake of his head. 'No, I'm not. You pounce on silly things I say. You button up if I lay a finger on you. *Why?* Is it just me you mistrust?—or all piano players?' he added wryly.

All men, Katya thought, not answering. *Or rather, not men but what they might turn me into, what they turned Vonnie into.*

He saw the shadow cross her face. 'Tell me,' Matt persisted in a gentle voice.

But she could not. 'I don't mistrust you,' she said with difficulty.

'No?' For an instant his fingers tightened round hers. Then—'So come home with me.'

It was a challenge, flung out coolly, and Katya gasped; she had not expected anything so forthright from him. His expression was unreadable. She suddenly had a conviction that her first instinctive response was wrong—that he was not, after all, inviting her home with the intention of seducing her, but that he was putting her to some sort of test.

She said cautiously, 'What for?'

A smile, the sudden charming self-mockery that she had already encountered and all but lost her heart to, appeared.

'Clever girl,' he said. 'I was thinking of food and listening to some of my new records. If that appeals?'

Katya drew a little breath of relief. So it *had* been a trap and she had not fallen into it.

'It appeals,' she said calmly. 'Let's go.'

Without comment he started swinging her hand as his pace increased and he started off rapidly in the direction of the river. Katya almost had to run to keep up with him. She was laughing and breathless by the time they reached the door in front of which he stopped.

Feeling for his key, he leaned forward at the same time and dropped a light kiss on the end of her nose.

'You're out of condition,' he told her with satisfaction, 'and out of breath. We've got six flights to climb. Shall I carry you?'

Katya made a face at him, for once not interpreting the remark as a preliminary to further flirtation. 'Just to prove that you *are* in condition?' She shook her head, the dark hair flying. 'I won't encourage you to show off. I shall get up there on my own if I have to do it on my hands and knees.'

'Right,' he said, laughing down at her. 'That's the last time I play the gentleman. On your own head— and hands and knees—be it.'

She followed him, and up the stairs, still laughing.

To her surprise the block was not a luxury apartment building. Indeed, except for rather better lighting on the stairs and more recently painted walls, it was not unlike her own.

She said as much on the second landing, while she still had the breath.

'No, I don't suppose there's much difference,' Matt agreed. 'Except that when they did this up they sound-proofed all the flats.'

'Sound-proofed?' gasped Katya. 'Though they didn't bother about carpeting the stairs or putting radiators in the hall, they *sound-proofed* the place?'

Matt looked amused. 'It was a necessity. It's a sort of musicians' commune, and when we're all practising it would sound like one of the torments of hell. It still does,' he added thoughtfully, 'in the afternoon when we've all got our windows open. Their imagination didn't run to air-conditioning.'

Katya was intrigued, 'Do you own the flat, then? I thought you were just staying briefly.'

His eyes mocked her. 'And unexpectedly. Yes, I am.

I've borrowed this from a friend of mine who teaches at the Conservatoire.'

'He's away?' Katya asked idly, knowing that most of the French people she was acquainted with took a holiday out of the city in August.

'No.' For a moment he seemed at a loss. 'No, but he doesn't live here. He just uses it to practise. So I—er—persuaded him that his bank balance would welcome a tenant. He comes back to practise every evening.'

'Doesn't he mind?' She was surprised. It didn't sound like an ideal arrangement from the friend's point of view, to have his practising hours telescoped into the evening like that.

'Yes,' Matt admitted. He threw her a swift glance. 'But I convinced him that my need was greater than his.'

'I see,' she said, though she didn't. 'Won't he be there now? Won't we disturb him?'

'No. Tonight he's giving a concert.'

He flung open the door to the apartment and stood back to allow Katya to precede him. She went in slowly.

The room was huge, that was the first thing she noticed, and like the stairway it had no carpet. The floorboards had been stained and highly polished to a honey-brown and a number of exotic rugs were scattered about. There was a gleaming grand piano at one end of the room, several upright chairs and a number of music stands grouped together under a window. Another, smaller, keyboard instrument, perhaps a harpsichord, stood in a corner, its top littered with sheet music and manuscript paper. Bookcases were lined with scores and bulging bundles of sheet music as well as books and files. There was also a fair amount of electrical paraphernalia and four huge speakers set strategically about the room, while one wall was lined with utilitarian shelving, holding what must have been hundreds of records and cassettes.

Katya had never been in such a room in her life. She stared round, fascinated.

'You *live* here?'

'Quite temporarily.' Matt closed the door softly. 'It's a bit Spartan, but it suits me for the moment. And it's the perfect place to work, if not to sleep.'

He indicated a solid couch in the far corner, covered with a thick Greek rug and bright cushions.

'Or to eat,' and he led the way into a tiny kitchen, no bigger than a ship's galley. 'Still, all the right cooking utensils are here and I promise you won't starve this evening. You'll just have to picnic.'

'I like picnics,' Katya said composedly.

'Good. So go and sit down or snoop or whatever you want to do while I prepare our picnic,' he told her briskly. He struck an attitude. 'I can't *bear* people in my kitchen while I cook.'

'Oh, you temperamental artists,' she mourned, teasing him.

She went back to the main room and wandered round, examining the books and scores, though she was careful not to move anything. On top of one of the speakers there was a fat bundle of typescript which she saw idly was full of words and not musical notation. Her eye registered the title page without interest, and then suddenly she recalled where she had heard the name before. She looked again. Yes, it was definitely the new Carrasco movie about Columbus.

She called out to him, 'What are you doing with the script of an unfinished film? Are you so much of a film buff, you read them before they hit the screen?'

Matt emerged from the kitchen, a blue-and-white striped butcher's apron swathed about him in workmanlike fashion.

'Oh you've found that, have you? Taken my invitation to snoop literally?' He sounded amused.

'I'm supposed to be doing the score for it, that's one of the reasons I'm locked away here. I've seen the rough cut; they've given me the script; I'm supposed to produce stirring themes while they're doing the final cutting.'

Katya frowned at the faintly contemptuous tone. 'Don't you like doing it?'

Matt shrugged. 'It pays the bills.'

'But——' She looked doubtfully at the typescript. 'Isn't it a great honour to be asked to write the score for a film like that? I mean a big prestige production of Carrasco's could surely have any composer it wanted.'

'Oh, sure, if you do it on merit alone.' He turned back to the kitchen but not before Katya had caught his expression of distaste. 'In this case, though, one or two strings were pulled on my behalf. I didn't know it was happening until too late, or I would have stopped it, but I couldn't hurt the person who set it up for me. So now I'm stuck with it.'

He disappeared, leaving Katya oddly disturbed. There were times when he seemed so cool, so able to handle anything that came his way. Yet at other times such as this, she sensed a bitterness, even rage, that she wanted obscurely to diffuse.

She picked up the script, flicking through it. Already well thumbed, it fell open at several places where someone, presumably Matt, had made marginal jottings. One scene, between the Queen of Castile and a messenger from Columbus, was heavily marked with three slashes and annotated, 'first use of love theme'.

She smiled, beginning to close the script. She did not think that Matt, with his cynicism and barely curbed impatience, was in much of a case to be writing love themes. She wondered who was playing the Queen and whether Matt would find inspiration in her performance. Curiously she turned to the first page, looking for a cast list.

It was there, of course. There was every reason why

it should be. And it told her not only who was playing the Queen, but why strings had been pulled to get Matt his commission and why he had been unable to turn it down. Because to do so would have hurt Steffy Solomon.

Katya went very still: there was, after all, no reason to be surprised. When they had first met he had been with Steffy and, though he said that the evening had been arranged by his agent, it had been obvious to Katya that Steffy had wanted him.

Which left the question: how did he feel about Steffy? And, with the beautiful, influential actress in his life, what did he mean by his determined pursuit of Katya herself? Above all, did she have the courage to ask him?

She was looking very serious when Matt came back into the room, carrying two tall glasses of greenish white wine. Crossing to her he offered her one and she took it mechanically, jumping at the impact of the icy glass.

'Careful,' he said unnecessarily. 'It's been in the fridge.'

She gave him a strained smile. 'You keep your glassware in the fridge?'

'One likes to be prepared.' He raised his glass to her in a mocking, silent toast. 'One never knows when a beautiful woman will walk in, after all. And in this weather it's unthinkable to drink cold wine out of lukewarm glasses.'

Katya's smile became even more strained. She sipped quickly, not answering. His brows twitched together.

'*Now* what have I said?' he asked resignedly.

'Do many beautiful women visit you here?' Katya asked lightly.

He was not deceived. 'So it's that again. The old Lothario image.' He reached out a hand and brushed her cheekbone very lightly. 'That was all a long time ago, honey. I've grown up since then.'

But, 'Do they?' she persisted.

His expression was ironic. 'No, they don't. When I'm working, people—all people—visit me by invitation and prior arrangement. If Helen of Troy turned up looking for tea and sympathy, I'd show her the door. Does that answer your question?'

And Steffy? Katya did not have the courage to ask, after all, she found.

Matt gave a soft, exasperated little laugh.

'Look, you're not a schoolgirl, you're a woman of twenty-four! You know the score. Sure, there have been other ladies in my life. I'm a lot older than you. But Bluebeard's gone out of fashion. They survived.'

Katya looked away. She knew she was being foolish. As he said, she was an adult. Surely she could handle a brief summer flirtation without all this heart-searching?

His next words confirmed her own thoughts. 'Take it one step at a time, hmm?' Again that fleeting caress of his finger against her skin. Katya gave a little shiver and he smiled. 'Forget the publicity and trust me. I promise I won't hurt you.'

In the days that followed he was as good as his word. He saw her every evening. Sometimes he would come to the science building to meet her and they would get into his hired car and drive out into the countryside for a long walk and a meal—or, as Katya teasingly said, sometimes a walk and a long meal, since Matt proved to be a connoisseur of small rural gourmet restaurants. Sometimes they would spend the evening in his apartment or hers, talking or listening to music. Sometimes they would simply sit together companionably, reading or working in friendly silence.

Under the influence of this undemanding lifestyle, Katya did slowly relax. The sexual tension was still there, of course, and she was honest enough to acknowledge it, but it was no longer paramount. Matt barely touched her.

This in itself puzzled and eventually disturbed her. She found herself tensing when his arm brushed hers accidentally in the kitchen, or if he gave her his hand to help her out of the car. And not because his touch was distasteful, either, but because she was conscious of a new and startlingly powerful desire that his hands would stay on her body, even that he would make love to her.

Katya was shaken by the discovery. She thought Matt knew it too, because once or twice she had surprised a quizzical look in her eyes as his hands fell away, and he scrupulously stepped back from her. She began to remind herself of his reputation, his past conquests, his much-publicised philosophy of no commitment and no regrets.

It was, she found, the only thing that made him angry. For some reason he could not bear her to mention the past events that had got him into the gossip columns.

'Judge for yourself,' he said once, brusquely, as they were driving through a twilit lane. 'If it seems to you that I'm the sort of man who gets drunk and smashes up bars, why do you come out with me?'

And Katya had no answer to that. The truth was, of course, that he did not seem to her to be that sort of person. He drank in moderation, but she never saw him the worse for alcohol. They went out to bars and restaurants and he never overturned a table or hit a waiter, though according to Dmitri's press-cuttings file, until a couple of years ago Matt had hardly been out for an evening without doing one or the other.

Dmitri, in fact, had proved officiously determined to open Katya's eyes to the true nature of her new escort. He regularly turned up on her doorstep with a batch of old cuttings in several languages and from magazines in three continents. Each one bore witness to Dmitri's theory that Matt was an unprincipled hellraiser. But as even Dmitri had to concede, they were all a couple of years out of date.

At first Katya was amused, then worried; eventually she grew angry.

'Look, he's a friend of mine, Dmitri,' she said roundly. 'Come and meet him one evening if you like, but stop trying to poison my mind against him, because you won't do it. All you'll do,' she added hardly, 'is convince me that I would be better not to see *you*.'

Dmitri refused the invitation and continued to issue dire warnings, but he grudgingly agreed that he would tell his librarian friend who had been researching Matt Saracen that she could stand down. No more press-cuttings were produced.

He did, however, warn her darkly that she was living in a fool's paradise. Matt Saracen was showing her only his gentlest side. They never went anywhere where they would meet his old friends, did they? He was lulling her, said Dmitri in a voice of dramatic foreboding, into a false sense of security. If only, he added, revealing an unsuspected knowledge of her family background, she would tell her grandparents and listen to their advice!

Katya, outraged, threw him out. He was, she said half-laughing but nevertheless really angry, a creep and a spy and she did not want him over her threshold until she had calmed down. He could look for someone else to fill any spare places in his Russian dance team. Katya was finished.

She told Matt about it that evening, expecting that he would laugh, as she had done after Dmitri had lumbered off in dignified sulks. Instead he looked troubled.

'Will he write to your grandfather do you think?' he asked.

Katya shrugged. 'Who knows? I suppose he's been sending them weekly reports anyway. Who cares?'

He said slowly, 'You cared so much that you ran away from them and wouldn't leave your address. What if they turn up in Paris now?'

'I shall hide behind you,' Katya said flippantly.

There was a little silence that was not flippant at all. She realised, in sudden and rising panic, that though the grey eyes had flared at her laughing remark, his gravity had not lifted.

Matt said, 'Come away with me.'

'*What?*' She was uncertain, off balance, still half-laughing.

'I've got to go to Vienna, a concert I can't get out of. Come too.'

She protested. 'Matt, I can't! My work—there's only two of us in the lab at the moment. If I go swanning off it means that Henri has to work ten hours a day without a break. It's not fair.'

His face was bleak. He turned away from her, his hands thrust deep into the pockets of his jeans.

'You don't trust me.' His tone was full of despair. 'Even now, after all . . .'

Katya said gently, 'It's got nothing to do with you. I simply cannot walk out of the laboratory at this juncture.' As he said nothing she added with impatience, 'Look, everyone else has taken his holiday now precisely *because* I said I'd be there covering for them all. I've given my word. Surely you can understand that?'

'Yes,' he said heavily, his eyes shadowed. 'Yes, but *you* don't understand. This could be our last chance before . . .' He broke off. 'Oh, *hell*.' He took an impatient step towards her. 'If you won't come with me, will you at least promise that you'll wait for me? That you won't do anything rash without talking to me first?'

Katya was bewildered. 'Matt, I——'

His hands grasped her roughly by the shoulders.

'Promise,' he said fiercely.

The intensity of it frightened her, but she knew that he was looking for a reassurance that, for some reason, he desperately needed. She leaned forward and kissed him. 'I promise,' she agreed quietly.

That last conversation troubled her. Even when he was in Vienna and telephoning in an apparently cheerful mood, she was concerned. There was something feverish in his cheerfulness. She wondered whether it was the tension of performing or whether some other, darker, emotion was driving him. In the end she decided it was probably the artistic temperament. After all, she reminded herself, she had never seen him when he was preparing for a performance.

He gave no clue in their telephone conversations. Katya grew increasingly restless.

The night before he was due home she could not sleep. She tossed and turned in the airless room, her head full of images of him, wishing only that he was with her. If they could only talk—or touch—then her restlessness would dissolve into peace, she felt. She slept fitfully and woke with tears on her face.

At last she abandoned the unequal struggle with her busy mind and got up and dressed. At this hour it was cooler than it would be for the rest of the day, she knew. Even so, Paris was already enveloped in a haze of warmth and dust and exhaust fumes. The articulated lorries rumbled past, the only vehicles moving at this hour. Katya let herself out of the building into the steaming early morning sun and began to walk rapidly.

She walked, or so it seemed to her, for miles. She walked until she was tired, her feet slipping in her sandals with perspiration. She walked while Paris began to wake. First the traffic increased, then the smell of baking filled the air and, finally, the little bakers' shops began to roll out their striped blinds and open their doors for business.

Katya bought a long baguette still hot from the oven, agreed with the friendly shopkeeper that it was going to be another hot day, and turned for home as the shadows shrank and lightened.

What was she going to do? She had never felt like this before, never felt so lost and empty when she was away from a man. Nor had she felt so agitated at the prospect of seeing anyone again. It was suddenly unendurable that she should have to wait until tonight. She needed to see Matt. She needed it now.

She would meet him at the airport. His flight arrived, he had told her, at eleven; she would be there. She would ring Henri and tell him that this was a crisis, that she was ill, anything. Indeed, the way she felt now neither was very far from the truth, thought the normally conscientious Katya.

Henri, when she finally roused him, was unsurprised.

'Get it sorted out, for God's sake,' he said wearily. 'Then perhaps you'll stop behaving like a jumping bean and the laboratory can become the nice quiet academic place it used to be.'

Katya gave a little laugh that broke in the middle, and thanked him.

The flight was late; the people disembarking looked busy and cross and hot. She hovered, suddenly uncertain. What if Matt wasn't pleased to see her? What if he was travelling with other people? He had never introduced her to his friends. He almost seemed to want to keep them apart. Perhaps he would not relish her invading his private time like this.

Three times she almost turned to go. Three times something, stronger than the fear of rejection, called her back. And at last she saw him.

He was alone. That much she registered at once without having to look carefully at the people walking beside him. He was in a brown study, frowning, apparently hardly aware of his surroundings. He looked tired, she noted with compassion.

She slipped through the crowd and caught up with him. Without saying anything she slid her hand round his on the handle of his overnight case, relieving him gently of the burden.

Matt stopped dead.

'*Katya!*'

She smiled. 'I thought you might care for a chauffeur,' she said lightly, disguising her over-whelming surge of feeling at the sight of him.

He relinquished the case and flung both arms round her in a bear-hug, sweeping her off her feet so that the case bumped against their legs and he staggered, laughing.

'Katya! Katya, darling. What are you doing here? I thought you couldn't leave your laboratory without committing mortal sin.'

His eyes were devouring her face, burning and for once without their habitual shadow. The warmth there dazzled her, but she kept her cool.

'So here I am in a state of mortal sin,' she teased.

Matt hugged her again, hard. She could feel his arms shaking with tension.

'Thank God for sin, then. Oh, it's so good to see you. I didn't dare to hope——' He broke off as the suitcase, dangling from her fingers still, banged hard against his shin. 'Damn it,' he said, looking down, 'have you come to meet me only to assault me? For God's sake, let's get rid of the luggage.'

Katya chuckled. 'I've got your car here. We can load it and then go wherever we like. I've got the rest of the day off.'

'*Have* you?' He released her from the circle of his embrace but retained a firm grasp on her right hand, transferring his suitcase into his other hand. 'That was uncharacteristically reckless.'

She made a face at him. 'Don't be smug. You work

as hard as I do, you just don't have to do it from nine to five.'

Matt laughed, playing a little tune with his fingers on the inside of the palm he held.

'I wasn't being smug. I was congratulating myself on my luck.'

Katya gave a little shiver at that secret, sensuous movement. But she was not going to admit it.

'Yes, finding taxis at this time of day can be hell,' she agreed innocently.

'And hopeless if you want to persuade the taxi-driver to take you to Fontainebleau so you can walk in the woods and snooze in the sun,' he agreed, solemn-faced.

'Is that what you're going to do?'

'It's what *we* are going to do,' he corrected. 'I've had enough of stuffy cities and people. I need some space. And quiet.' His glance slewed round to her. 'And you,' he added quietly, so quietly she almost didn't hear it.

They found a quiet glade by a little stream where branches met overhead and filtered the sunlight to dusty gold. Matt slipped off his jacket and rolled it up into a pillow for Katya. She stretched out, watching him, while he sat with his back against an old beech tree and tipped his head back in luxurious relaxation.

She suddenly realised how very strained he had looked at the airport.

'Hard work?' she asked him. 'Vienna, I mean.'

He glanced down at her. 'Not particularly.'

'You're looking very tired, though.'

The grey eyes glinted. 'Are you asking me whether I've been on the town?'

'No.' It had not occurred to her, and she looked at him in genuine surprise. 'I just thought you looked worn out—as if it had taken too much out of you.'

Matt was still for a moment. 'Maybe it has, at that,' he said at last.

Katya reached out a comforting hand. After an instant's hesitation his own closed over it.

'Are the Viennese audiences so difficult, then?'

'No.' He drew a long sigh and his eyes changed, as if he were looking somewhere far removed from the peaceful clearing. 'No, rather the reverse. And I played better too. But——'

He broke off. Katya could see that he was no longer with her. The fine brows contracted as he stared across the little stream with an almost grim expression. She gave their clasped hands a twitch.

'But . . .?'

Matt turned back to her with a start. He's forgotten me, she thought, part amused, part forlorn.

'I don't know that I can explain it,' he said eventually, looking down at their hands. 'I don't understand it myself.'

'Try,' she urged softly.

'All right.' He tipped his head back against the bark again. The coppery hair caught the light like a jewel set in wood. Katya found herself startled by the beauty of it; and of the fine-boned face, even in its tiredness and bewilderment.

She swallowed.

'It's as if I'm not in charge of the music any more,' Matt said slowly. 'Can you understand that?'

She shook her head.

'Well, I've always been a super-technician. Whatever else they might have said, my worst enemy couldn't have faulted my technique. And now——' he half-laughed, as if he was ashamed of what he was going to say '—it's like it's running away with me. Mistiming, rough edges, false notes ... all the mistakes I stopped making when I was eighteen.'

Katya stared. 'But you said you were playing better.'

'Yes, I am.' He was not impatient with her ignorance. If anything he was slightly rueful. 'I know that must seem like a nonsense to you, when I've just told you my technique is failing.'

'It doesn't sound very sensible,' she admitted.

Matt swung round to face her. 'Katya, do you know what was wrong with my playing? Did you realise?'

'Why, I—the critics—you said you might practise too much,' she floundered. 'I told you, I'm not very musical.'

'The real trouble was that there wasn't any heart to it. As my technique got better I seemed to lose all feeling for the music.' He grimaced. 'At least, that's one theory. Another is that I was so overloaded with feeling in my family life that I shut it out of everywhere else. I don't know whether either—or even both—could be true. But there's no doubt than any profundity went out of my playing when I was in my mid-twenties. The sound came out like a miraculously engineered musical box,' he added, with vivid bitterness.

Moved, Katya raised their entwined hands to her cheek and cradled his fingers in silent sympathy.

'And now I don't know what's happened or why. I haven't made any changes—at least not deliberately. I'm probably practising less, but not a lot less. But somehow—suddenly—I'm not a brilliant engineer any more. I'm a real man playing music he feels.' His fingers moved against her cheek convulsively. 'And making elementary mistakes to prove it.'

'Do you mind?' she asked quietly. 'The mistakes, I mean.'

Matt shrugged. 'Not if they're the price I have to pay. I should be able to work them out of my system eventually, anyway.'

'Then why are you so—disturbed?'

He turned fully towards her and flung himself down on his front, holding their clasped hands between them as if they were playing some childish trial of strength. His eyes were very sober, though.

'Because I'm out of control. Surely you can understand that? You're a very self-possessed lady. I don't like feeling as if I'm bobbing about on a high sea with no direction and no way of righting myself if I go under.'

It was so much what she had felt herself, that something twisted inside Katya. He saw it in her face, for his hand tightened.

'Yes, you *do* understand that, don't you?' He looked away. 'I'm playing well now: I don't know why. Tomorrow I might play badly: I wouldn't know why that happened either. I'm frightened, Katya,' he ended in a low voice.

With an inarticulate murmur she wriggled round beside him, taking him into her arms with an ease that, in retrospect, astonished her. It was as if she was used to comforting Matt in this way; had done so many times before. His head dropped against her breast with a little sigh.

'I wish I'd been there,' she murmured, torn with remorse when she remembered that he had asked her to go with him and she had rejected him. 'I wish you hadn't been alone.'

Matt said quietly, 'I don't think I've ever felt alone—really alone—since I met you.'

Katya sat very still. Somewhere among the leaves a thrush was singing, beauty tumbling from its busy throat. Insects whirred, the little stream splashed against the stones that forded it. Branches stirred. The very air seemed to hum with warmth and life. She felt as if they were in an enchanted place, in an enchanted moment, and any sudden move or word would spoil it.

Matt turned, very gently, and pulled her down on to the fragrant grasses. She stared up at him in a daze. The light refracted from a lock of Titian hair split into a shimmering rainbow. Katya put up a dreamy hand to touch it.

Matt said, 'Can you understand that, too?'

'Yes.' It was little more than a sigh, shy, bewildered and reluctant.

His mouth twisted. 'I don't think you can, you know. Oh, you're solitary all right, I've seen that, but you don't know about the loneliness of the soul, when you're surrounded by people none of whom care and none of whom matter.'

'Hush. It's over.'

'Is it?' Matt was sombre.

'It would be,' she whispered, 'if you stopped talking and kissed me.'

His eyes gleamed. 'You may be right at that,' he murmured, before he lowered his head and complied.

For long silvery seconds, Katya hardly breathed, savouring him with every sense. Time stopped as their bodies moved against each other without urgency, filled only with a sense of peace and absolute rightness. His hands moved delicately in her hair. His lips on her skin were a languorous delight she had never imagined.

He drew away, at last, one hand still on the soft muslin skirt at her hip. He looked down at her, his eyes tender.

'You're magic, do you know that? Kind and clever and beautiful—and you make me feel again. Just as I used to do when I was young.'

'And you're so old now,' she teased, violet eyes warm with shared affection.

'Compared with you, I am, my darling.' And when she protested, 'In experience at least.'

She was so happy she refused to be intimidated by his doubts.

'So your experience will teach you how to value all this,' she said blithely, ruffling his hair.

'Oh, it does.' He feathered a kiss across her parted lips. In its very lightness the caress was infinitely sensual. 'It's not me who undervalues it.'

Katya gave a little sigh of pure satisfaction. 'Well, I

certainly don't. Look at me, giving up a whole day's work for it,' she pointed out with mischief.

'True.' Matt laughed down at her. Then, as their eyes met, the world stilled and the laughter died, giving place to fiercer, deeper emotions.

The trees swung and dipped before her unfocusing eyes and she reached for Matt in undisguised need. Passion flared as he sought her mouth, not with gentle teasing now. He strained her to him, bone against bone, pulse against leaping pulse. The hunger she had always sensed in him was there now, naked in the harsh breathing, the seeking mouth and the impetuous, impatient hands.

And suddenly, in that totally adult hunger, he had left her behind. She was no more than a cautious child with a toe in the water who suddenly looks up to see a giant wave about to crash over her; she could not prevent the flash of fear, the instinctive recoil. And Matt felt it.

At once the bruising arms relaxed, though he did not wholly release her. He lifted his mouth from hers and stayed for a moment, head bent, resting on the arms that imprisoned her body. Katya saw that his chest was rising and falling as if he had run a race.

She said in a small voice, 'I'm sorry.'

Matt raised his head then and looked at her. The grey eyes were nearly black, but the mouth wore the rueful self-mocking smile that she was coming to love.

'I think I'm the one who ought to be apologising. I knew you didn't want to be rushed.'

'You're very—understanding,' she muttered, furious with herself.

He touched one long finger to her hot cheek. 'Don't look like that, my darling. There's nothing wrong.'

'I'm so *stupid* . . .'

But he put his hand over her mouth before she could continue.

'You are what you are and so am I, and in time we'll

know each other better. For the moment,' he stroked her lower lip with his thumb, 'I'm enjoying the journey of discovery. Why don't you do the same?'

She was so filled with gratitude and affection that she almost told him she loved him; she almost believed it. Almost.

CHAPTER SIX

AFTER that, though, Katya stopped pretending to herself that Matt was a passing interest of no long-term importance in her life. She was not at all sure what she was to him, but she knew that whatever happened between them now, she had already been irreparably changed by the relationship. She had never felt so close to somebody, so at home. She said as much to him one evening as they wandered along by the river under the shadow of the Eiffel Tower.

Matt looked down at her. 'That's hardly surprising,' he said. 'You've never let yourself feel at home with anyone at all, from what I gather.'

Katya gave a theatrical sigh. 'You're going to start telling me off again for my solitary lifestyle, I can hear it in your voice.'

His smile was reluctant. 'No, I'm not, though you deserve it. No, it's deeper than that. You've let your family, or rather your grandparents, build a wall so high round you that you can't see over it.'

Katya was offended. 'I got away from them, didn't I?'

'Ran away,' Matt corrected, 'making sure they couldn't trace you.' Katya had told him all about the elaborate arrangements she had made to receive her mail so that her grandparents didn't discover that she was in Paris rather than another, provincial, French city. 'And barred the gate against everyone else at the same time.'

'I don't know what you're talking about.'

'No? Well, answer me this, then: how many friends have you got in London?'

Katya shrugged. 'A couple. Old school friends, people I knew at college.'

'Who write to you? Who visit you? Who care about you when you're down?'

She stared at him. 'I suppose not,' she said slowly.

'Exactly.'

They walked on in silence for a while. Katya frowned over the river, her hand unresponsive in Matt's light clasp.

At last she said, 'What is it that you're trying to tell me, Matt?'

'I'm not sure. Perhaps just to try to make you realise how very—unusual you are.' He stopped and turned to face her. 'Most people don't have to run away from home to make their point, you know.'

Katya sniffed. 'Most people don't have grandparents like mine, with one foot in Imperial Russia. I had to demonstrate that I was self-sufficient . . .'

'That's precisely what I mean,' he pounced. '*Self*-sufficient. When you cut out your grandparents, you cut out everybody else as well. And while it might be brave, that's not a very sensible thing to do.'

Katya disengaged her fingers and walked on. Matt fell into step beside her, not speaking. She bit her lip as she turned his words over in her mind.

Was he right? More, why was he saying it? She had said that she had never felt so close to anyone before. Was he telling her—as kindly as possible—that was simply because of her solitary lifestyle? That he, running his life in a different way, found nothing unique in their relationship?

She looked at him doubtfully from under her lashes. Of course he must have had lots of affairs, with those devastating brooding looks and his charm. It didn't need ancient gossip columns or Dmitri Kolkanin to convince her of that. And although he seemed totally absorbed in her now, that *was* now, and he never mentioned the future. Perhaps he expected to move on when his time in Paris ended, leaving them both with a charming memory and no scars. Katya shivered, suddenly cold.

'Hey, don't look like that,' Matt admonished gently. 'It's not the end of the world. You're young; you've still got plenty of time to build a life with room for other people in it.'

Katya's lips stretched in a strained smile. 'And put my mistakes behind me?'

'Put your mistakes where you can learn from them,' Matt temporised, slipping his arms round her waist and drawing her back close to his side again. 'That's what mistakes are for.'

She nearly asked him whether he thought this friendship of theirs would come in the category of mistakes in the end. But, though he had called her brave, she didn't have the courage.

So she walked on beside him in the dusty Paris evening, watching the Seine slide like an oiled animal under the bridges. Matt was perfectly at home in Paris, more so than she was, though she had lived there for more than two years. She had the feeling that he would make himself at home in any city in the space of time it took him to unpack his suitcase and get out among the streets. Perhaps he did not need his roots to go very deep, she thought desolately.

Matt said abruptly, 'It's emotional blackmail, you know.'

Her thoughts were so far away that Katya jumped and, for a moment, thought he was accusing her of something.

'What?'

'Emotional blackmail,' he repeated, 'what your grandparents do. You should never have given in to it. Blackmailers get more powerful the more you meet their demands. You should have made a stand once and for all.'

'When?' asked Katya tiredly. 'When I was at school? That was big enough concession already in their eyes; and Vonnie was ill, too.'

He looked down at her sharply. She lifted her shoulders in answer to his unspoken question.

'I don't really know what was wrong with her. It was all terribly hushed up, with Grandmama looking like a saint and trying not to cry all the time. I suppose it was some sort of nervous breakdown. How could I have made any sort of stand against them when they were having to cope with that?'

Matt said softly, 'You love them.'

Katya shook her head. 'I'm not sure that I do. They're not easy to love, either of them: Grandmama's so formal and my grandfather is so absolutely unpredictable that he's more like a phenomenon of the weather than a person. But—I can't help seeing that they were already old when they took Vonnie in, and then, when my parents were killed, it must have been the last straw. Even if they hadn't been as they were, it would have been a terrific strain for them at their age.'

'You're too kind. It made it too easy for those two egocentric old monsters to prey on you,' Matt said.

He spoke with such coldness that Katya was shocked. Her eyes flew to his face, finding it closed and implacable.

'How can you say that?'

'I can say it because I know very well the damage they've done, not only to you,' he said grimly. 'And all to feed their vanity; their own ridiculous ideas of what is due to them and their rank, without a thought for what it costs other people, including their own family. I've no patience with them.'

'No, I can see that,' Katya agreed wryly. 'I didn't realise you'd known them so well.'

'I guess I saw a lot of the broken pieces.' Matt was sombre.

'When you knew Paul at Oxford?' Katya ventured, disturbed by his face of bitter memories.

'I—yes,' he said after a hesitation, 'when I knew Paul.' His arm tightened round her waist and he began to urge them forward faster. 'And I'm glad you got away. Perhaps you're right: perhaps the only way you

could escape from those two spiders was by flight.
Let's forget them. Let's go and find lots of people and
dance till dawn and behave like students again.'

Katya laughed, almost running in the circle of his
arm.

'I didn't spend my student days with lots of people
dancing till dawn,' she protested.

'Then you should have,' Matt said, unmoved, 'I
did. Now's your time to catch up.' He swung her
round in front of him, off her feet, while she laughed
at him and told him to put her down, drumming her
fists on his chest in mock protest. He leered at her.
'Let me show you a good time, baby.'

'Oh stop it,' said Katya, dazed as much by her
precarious position as by this sudden change of mood.
'If I laugh any more I shall get a stitch.'

'Not until you promise to dance the night through
with me.'

An elderly couple approaching them along the
pavement pulled out and took a wide detour to avoid
them. They stared as they passed, their expressions
mingled disapproval and alarm.

'Put me down,' begged Katya, embarrassed.

Matt had seen them too. He raised his voice
wickedly. 'Only if you promise to give me what I
want,' he said in tones that must have carried to them.

The elderly couple accelerated their pace.

'All right. All *right*!'

Katya was lowered to the ground. She shook out the
skirts of her dress and ran fingers through her
disarranged hair, trying to look reproachful.

'Now look what you've done! They'll probably go
off and report you to the police for mugging or
something.'

Matt was undisturbed. 'That'll be a new one for the
gossip columns,' he said tranquilly.

And, sweeping his arm round her with that easy
intimacy, he took her off to a student cellar where he

made a very creditable attempt to do as he had said he would. It was only Katya, protesting that she had to be at work at a reasonable hour the next morning, who persuaded him to leave at half-past two. He saw her home ceremoniously, kissed her lightly at her door and then went off, announcing blithely that he was not sleepy and intended to work.

Katya shut her door slowly, hearing him run down the stairs, his energy lending credibility to his intention. His work seemed to be going well, she thought. He hardly spoke of it but when they met he looked alert and well-satisfied and when she asked him about his film score he would say with a small, secret smile, that it was 'coming along'. So in spite of the time he was spending with her he did not seem to be slacking, which was something of a relief. For he was spending a very great deal of time with her.

Too much, according to Dmitri, waiting gloomily on the steps of the chemistry building when she came out one evening.

'They think he has gone to ground, that he is having a secret affair,' Dmitri told her portentously, having acquired her briefcase and with it, the privilege of escorting her home.

Katya seized her briefcase from his hand.

'Oh, look, I've had enough of this! I don't want to hear your poison about Matt. Do you understand me? I don't want to listen to unfounded malice.'

And she strode away from him angrily.

He shouted after her, 'See if he will take you to the Meurice opening. See if it is unfounded gossip.'

Katya did not look back or answer. She was too angry.

By the time she got home, though, she had cooled. She didn't believe Dmitri's tissue of gossip and supposition, of course. She was sure that Matt would not deceive her in that way. Though there was something—she had long been aware of it and it still niggled worryingly at the back of her mind—that he was keeping from her, she was sure of it. And yet—and yet——

When Matt arrived that night she was tense and trying to disguise it. He noticed at once.

'What's this? Housework?' he remarked, running his hand over her newly tidied and polished desk. 'Are you worrying about something?'

'I—no, of course not. Don't be ridiculous.'

'You're not normally so domestic,' he pointed out reasonably.

'I just had time, and thought I'd make the place look a little less like a scribe's cell,' Katya said, trying to sound relaxed.

'I don't believe you,' Matt returned calmly, swinging gently in her revolving chair. 'Come here.'

She went. Of course, she went. She always did these days. The welcome, welcoming warmth of his embrace was becoming as familiar and as necessary to her as the air she breathed. He gathered her comfortably against him.

'Tell.' And when she did not speak, 'Is it us?'

'A—a little.'

Matt sighed. 'You're not going to tell me we're going too fast, I hope. I'm taking it so slow, I'm practically stationary.'

'No—no. No, it's not that.'

'What, then?' he asked with patience.

Katya bit her lip. 'Matt, I don't really fit in with your life, do I?'

He stared at her. She had the feeling that, whatever it was that he had been expecting, and he had certainly been braced for something, it wasn't that.

'What do you mean, fit in?'

She made a wide gesture. 'With your friends, for instance. You never take me to see your friends.'

'I'm not seeing my friends myself. I'm working whenever I'm not with you.'

'But that's my point, don't you see? If you were in Paris working on your own, you wouldn't be spending every evening away from your old friends.'

'Say rather my old haunts,' Matt answered wryly. 'No, if I wasn't seeing you, I'd probably be in some bar most nights. *And* sleeping off the results instead of working the next day,' he added. 'So you've been a good influence on me.' He kissed her lingeringly. 'How does it feel to be a good influence?'

'Rather dreary,' Katya said ruefully.

He held her away from him. 'You mean it, don't you?'

She shrugged. 'It's probably just a silly idea. Forget it. Tell me about Columbus.'

He ignored the reference to his film score. 'No, this is serious.' He touched her cheek lightly. 'Especially if it drives you into polishing the woodwork as therapy. We'll go on a bar-crawl if that's what it takes to reassure you, though I expect you'll be heartily bored.'

Katya said carefully, 'Does it have to be a bar-crawl? Couldn't we go to that new discothèque? I've heard it's going to have a fantastic opening. Couldn't you get an invitation?'

This time Matt really stared at her, his eyes narrowed, his hands stilled against her tense shoulders. 'You want to go to the Meurice?'

'Can't we?' Katya tried to instil a note of wistful enthusiasm into her voice and was not satisfied with the result.

'Oh, we *could* easily enough. I've already been asked. But you don't like discos.'

'But you're always telling me I ought to change and broaden my horizons,' Katya pointed out.

'And you want to broaden them as far as Reynaud's new nightspot?' Matt sounded weary and just a little suspicious. But in the end he shrugged. 'All right, if that will make you feel that you fit into my life, as you say. Though I'm not sure that that's the sort of life I want to fit into myself any more.'

So they went. Katya was relieved that Dmitri's prediction that Matt would refuse to take her had been unfounded. Of course she hadn't really believed Dmitri, but still she had wondered. It was good to know that Dmitri was wrong in this, as he probably was in all the other things he'd said.

Meanwhile she had to maintain pretended enthusiasm for the treat. She loved dancing but not the modern gyrations, and she had never been to a discothèque in her life and was slightly alarmed at the prospect. Having insisted on going, however, she couldn't admit as much to Matt. She did to Babette Leon, though.

Babette was highly amused. She was watching the progress of Katya's first major relationship since she had known her with some interest. At first she had been a little worried—now, however, she thoroughly approved. And a frivolous night on the town, dressed to the nines and dancing till dawn, exactly appealed to her sense of what was fitting for young lovers.

'Don't be foolish,' she advised robustly. 'Flat pretty shoes that you can keep dancing on for hours and a cool dress with lots of sparkle. It's easy.'

Katya looked, if anything, even more alarmed.

'I will help,' said Babette. 'I told you a long time ago you could be devastating if you wanted to be. Well, now you want to be, I think?' and she raised a quizzical eyebrow.

Katya thought of all the fashionable lovelies that would be at the Meurice opening and felt her heart sink. Perhaps it had been to her advantage that Matt had not taken her among that group of his friends; she was not going to be able to compete. Perhaps when he saw her against that backdrop he would realise how very ordinary she was.

She said in a voice she did not recognise, 'I want to be as devastating as you know how, Babette.'

Her friend laughed. 'Excellent! Then first we go shopping. Then, we try some little things with that lovely hair. Then the make-up. It will,' she warned, 'take a lot of time.'

It did. Katya did not have a lunch hour for a week in which she did anything but trot from shop to shop in Babette's competent wake. At the end of it, she found herself with a filmy tunic, cut away daringly at the back and under the arms, with a long swathe of trailing convolvulus undulating across it in brilliant beadwork, pointed shoes with sparkling buckles and the paint to produce, if she chose, a whole new face.

Babette, however, was wise enough to avoid extremes of make-up, though she piled Katya's hair high, letting just a few curling wisps lie against the young neck, and secured it with glittering combs. Staring at herself in the mirror, Katya was pleased and faintly appalled. She looked like a jazz baby, she told Babette, not like herself.

'But perhaps a hidden part of you *is* a jazz baby,' Babette picked up her bag and prepared to leave. 'Have a good time finding out.'

When she had gone Katya leaned forward, peering: her eyes, though only lightly shadowed with a spectrum of colours by Babette's skilful fingers, looked huge and hungry. The perfect skin was just dusted over with a shimmery powder that made her look, she thought, theatrical and a little unreal. And her mouth, tremulous under shading and gloss, was the least recognisable thing about her: full, with a promise of sensuality to which she was a stranger.

She gave a quick, light shiver. She did not look like herself but she did look like one of the girls that Matt knew so well. Had he brought about this transformation? Had she really changed?

It startled Matt too. When he arrived a few minutes later, he stared at her as if she were a vision he was half repelled by.

'Won't I do?' Katya asked nervously, when he did not speak. 'Will you be ashamed of me?'

'I'm more likely to spend the evening hauling men off you,' Matt said slowly. 'What have you done to yourself?'

'Don't you like it?' she asked, disappointed.

He hesitated. 'It's not a question of liking. It's——' He broke off and then said, the grey eyes serious, 'You do realise how sexy you look?'

Katya felt colour rise in her cheeks and turned away in embarrassment. He took her by the shoulders.

'No, don't look away. I'm not paying you silly compliments. It isn't just that you're beautiful. You're always beautiful. It's just that tonight—for the first time since I've known you—you look as if you've come out of your time capsule and into the real world.' He trailed the back of his hand down her bare arm, watching her shiver as he did so. 'Available,' Matt said levelly, 'that's what you look. Bear it in mind, this evening. It can't often happen to you.'

He was in an odd mood, she thought, confused—not hostile, exactly, but prickly—and he didn't get any easier after they arrived at the nightclub and joined a party who hailed him almost as soon as they entered. Though she talked—as well as she could for the music was very loud—and was friendly to them and danced all the time with his friends, his mood did not lighten at all.

The music grew louder as the evening wore on. Katya glanced at Matt in concern, wondering whether his musical sensitivity was offended by it, but he appeared unmoved. He was dancing with a spiky-haired girl in clown's baggy pants and jacket with what seemed very likely to be nothing underneath. Her face had been painted ghost-pale and showed no animation, though her body flickered around Matt with the vitality of a stalking jaguar. Katya saw him laugh as the girl seized his hand and whirled herself against him, her gyrating shoulders touching his chest, her exotic face tipped up to him over her shoulder.

The whole pose invited a kiss and more. Katya lowered her eyes rapidly. She did not want to see Matt kiss a girl on the dance floor, however little it might matter. And it did *not* matter, she told herself painfully, they both knew it didn't. It was one of the conventions of the disco way of life.

But she had momentarily lost her concentration. The man beside her continued to boast about his 1938 roadster and she continued to smile mechanically but suddenly she had become an outsider, watching. Her eyes roved round the room. The people were weirdly dressed, some beautifully, and the hectic gaiety felt oppressive. It was almost contrived. Katya had been taken by Dmitri to a photographic session where the models had all danced and laughed and caressed to piped music while he photographed them; the moment he finished the music was turned off, the models subsided glumly into varying states of exhaustion and divested themselves of their finery as quickly as possible.

That was what this club reminded her of, she now realised. As if it was some giant performance, all the partygoers looked as if they too would slump into silence the moment the cameras stopped. It made her uneasy. She scanned the room, looking for just one face that looked as if it was genuinely enjoying itself.

And stopped, with a gasp.

For in a corner, though hardly out of the limelight, looking like a creature from another world in simulated tiger-skin so brief that it was barely respectable, was her cousin Vonnie. The black hair was free and flying wildly as she danced; her wonderful Caribbean tan had been dusted over with glitter so that she looked as if she was made of gold crystal. Her eyes were outlined by a thick Cleopatra line and the lids painted like stained glass in irregular patches of bright colours. Katya shook her head. She was Vonnie and yet, looking like this in these surroundings, not Vonnie. Her cousin could only stare.

Vonnie, finishing a dance and waving away her partner as if he were a waiter who had given her a glass of wine, looked up and at once her eyes narrowed on Katya. A look of disbelief crossed the lovely face, and then a smile. She raised an arm in greeting and strolled across the dance floor.

'Hi,' she said generally to the others at Katya's table and slid along the bench-seating next to her cousin. 'What are you doing here, sweetie? I thought you were toiling in the bowels of some university and waiting for the Nobel Chemistry Prize.'

Katya, who recognised her grandfather's inflated reporting behind this account, laughed. 'That's just by day,' she assured Vonnie.

Her cousin leaned back, sliding both arms out along the back of the velvet-covered seat and looked at her. The lashes were huge and false like something out of a cartoon. Vonnie did not look her age, which was ten years older than Katya. She did not look any age, Katya realised. She looked completely alien, except for that lazy twinkle which was wholly Vonnie.

'So by night you turn into a werewolf,' drawled Princess Irena. 'Quite a comely werewolf at that.'

Katya pulled a face. 'I think I look weird.'

'So who doesn't?' Vonnie lifted a shoulder disparagingly. 'This is the outer reaches of style, pet.' She fluttered the outrageous lashes and grinned. 'How do you like it?'

'Great for a tonic, not much for a regular diet,' Katya said promptly.

'Bit too much fizz,' her cousin agreed nonchalantly. 'Still, it's great to see you taking more fizz with it. You've been an upright citizen quite long enough!'

Katya chuckled affectionately. 'You're not the only one who thinks so.'

'I hear the echo of a guy who fancies you,' said Vonnie with amusement. 'Is that why he brought you here?'

Katya shook her head. 'No, it was my idea. I thought I could do with some pepping up.'

'Good for you. So he just came along for the ride. Who is he?'

But Katya, though she loved Vonnie and trusted her, found she did not want to tell. 'Over there,' she said vaguely, gesturing in the direction of Matt and his partner and a dozen or so others.

Vonnie did not press her. She looked mildly interested, and then said, 'He must be a friend of Reynaud's. They're all here, Crispin and La Plage and Steffy Solomon. So I suppose Saracen will be as well, though I haven't seen him.' There was an odd note in her voice.

Katya said quickly, 'Have you seen Steffy Solomon, then?'

'Oh yes, almost as soon as I arrived. She knows I never go to London if I can help it, so she brought me the new Langridge catalogue.' She made a face. 'Not that it's all that new any more. She must have got it when she was staying with Saracen in June. Their autumn catalogue will be out soon.'

Katya felt as if her cousin had accidentally broken a glass, and one of the shards had flown up and pierced her to the heart. Vonnie was still talking. She had not noticed her cousin's sudden rigidity. How could she know that in that one careless sentence she had opened up more suppressed doubts in Katya's mind than all Dmitiri's calculated accusations had done? She had no idea that it was Matt Saracen who had brought her cousin here this evening; no idea that it was her cousin's presence in Paris that had brought him to the city.

Katya felt the hurt like a physical pain. Every time she looked at Matt, now dancing with a pretty girl with green hair who was draped in what appeared to be a tennis net, it stabbed at her again. Staying with Saracen in June. Just a few weeks ago they must have been lovers. Yet now . . .

'Yes,' she said blindly when the man beside her took her hand and tugged at it, to take her on to the dance floor.

Vonnie was smiling, waving, caught up herself by a couple of bare-chested young men in Oriental trousers.

'I'm off to Florida tomorrow but I'll ring the next time I'm in Paris,' she called, as heads swirled between them and they all began to dance to the insistent drumbeat.

Katya danced for hours. She moved like an automaton, not enjoying it, not disliking it. It was something to do which kept her away from Matt and the awareness of how recently he had belonged to somebody else.

It could not last, of course. Eventually he was before her, among the stamping dancers, the handsome face tense as he took her hand. 'Time we went home.'

Katya said, resisting, 'Why? Nobody else is going yet.'

Matt looked weary. 'People are coming and going all the time.'

'Well, the place is still full.'

'It will stay full till six but we aren't going to be among the fools who are here when they put out the trash,' Matt stated.

He danced her away from the centre of the floor, strewn now with the remains of balloons and trailing twirls of coloured paper. He found her bag and his jacket, raised a casual hand to a couple who called out to him, and got her up the stairs and into the air.

It was not cold, indeed, it was one of the stuffiest

nights of that heavy summer. But the nightclub had
been overheated by all the bodies and their agitation:
outside came as a shock, and Katya shivered. At once,
without asking her, Matt swung his jacket which he
had looped from a finger, over her shoulders. Katya
accepted it mutely.

In the car they said nothing. Nor did he speak as,
after they had tiptoed up to her room, he eschewed his
usual practice of kissing her good night and leaving
her. Silently he unlocked the door, ushered her inside
and came too, closing it behind him and leaning his
shoulders against it.

Katya walked away from him, oddly breathless, and
turned to face him. Though she could not explain it
she felt almost like an animal at bay. Matt looked
down at her enigmatically, the cheekbones prominent,
the eyes steel-hard beneath their heavy lids.

Katya moistened her lips nervously. 'It's—it's very
late, Matt.'

The glint of gunmetal grey as his eyes flashed
increased her nervousness.

'I'm very tired. Thank you for taking me, but I
ought to go to bed now.'

He did answer that, in an even tone which did
nothing to dispel her mounting anxiety. 'Yes, we
probably ought.'

She tried a light laugh; not very convincingly. 'You
don't mean that.'

'You think not?' A thin eyebrow rose in interest.
Still he had not moved. 'Come here,' he said softly.

Something substantial seemed to have wedged itself
in Katya's throat, and she swallowed hard. 'I've got to
get up early tomorrow, Matt. It's my turn to be in
first.'

He gave her a slow smile. 'I'll get you up in time,'
he promised.

Katya stopped trying to behave with dignity and
retired behind her swivel chair. 'I'd like you to go

now, please, Matt,' she said rapidly. 'I've had a very pleasant evening but I want to be alone now.'

He said, with apparent irrelevance, 'Your cousin was there tonight. Did you talk to her?'

Katya closed her eyes, hoping the pain did not show. 'Yes.'

'And now you want to send me away?'

'I do, yes,' she told him steadily.

He shook his head, quite gently. 'No way. I've stepped like a cat round your inhibitions, your upbringing, your dictatorial grandparents, and no silly butterfly like your cousin Vonnie is going to louse things up now.'

Katya stared at him, her mouth dry. 'I don't know what you mean.'

'I mean that you came down to earth tonight, sweetheart. And that's exactly where you're staying.'

He crossed the room and took the chair away from her clutching hands. His jacket slid from her shoulders as he reached for her, his hands warm on her shivering skin.

'I told you you looked sexy in that thing,' Matt reminded her, a gleam of amusement appearing briefly, 'and you do. Christian could hardly keep his hands off you.' He was running his fingers up and down her exposed spine, flexing them without impatience but with an absolute assurance that told her that he did not mean to be gainsaid. 'And now I don't have to,' he said thickly, as his head lowered.

With a little sigh, Katya went limp. Her head was thrown back in abandon. Matt kissed her ferociously, his tongue deep in her mouth, as if there was no part of her he would not seek out and master. As they stood there he freed her from the glittering dress, and it fell to her feet with a soft hush. Neither noticed.

This was what she wanted. Oh God, this was all she wanted, to be close to him, closer than mouth to mouth, holding and wanting and sharing that searing want until it consumed them both. She gave a little sob as he released her mouth and plundered a trail of sensation with his kisses along her arching throat to the tender fluttering pulse. Blindly she cradled his head against her, moved by the sweetness, the strangeness of it. Matt drew in his breath sharply.

'Do you want me to make love to you?' he asked, his mouth moving against her skin.

Katya was shaken almost beyond words, but that gave her pause. He felt the hesitation, he must have done, for he dropped his mouth to one lifting breast, using his tongue and lips to persuade her without words. She was trembling like a reed, her eyes wide and anguished under that slow, deliberate tease.

'You're very alluring when you can't make up your mind,' Matt murmured, laughter in his voice. Then he took her hand and turning his head suddenly, pressed a warm kiss into the palm, and closed her fingers over it as if to hold it safe.

'Oh, *Matt*,' Katya said, wanting to give him everything.

He picked her up easily and took her across to the bed, smiling. As he lowered her she looked up at him in a rush of anxiety, blushing a little.

'Matt, you won't expect too much of me? I'm not like Vonnie. I don't know . . .'

He kissed her hard, stopping the sentence with his mouth.

'For God's sake, that's why we're here. Can't you realise, you silly girl, you're not a shadow of Vonnie— or a toy for your grandmother to play with either, for that matter? You're your own person. If I can't make you understand it any other way, I will tonight.'

It sounded almost like a vow. Katya faltered, the lovely sensuous glow he had brought to her beginning to die as his words began to make themselves felt.

'You mean you want to take me to bed to prove a point? As a sort of therapy?' she asked slowly.

'Hell!' It was a savage sound, so unlike him that she jumped and flinched back. His hands fell away. 'You can't be that innocent, surely? You must know why I want to take you to bed.'

She tried to smile. 'Yes, you told me earlier. That dress.'

'Don't be a fool,' Matt said cryptically. He drew back. 'I get the feeling that you've changed your mind, Princess.'

Katya bit her lip, looking away. She was very cold now, shivering inside and slightly sick, but she knew that she had encouraged him, lured him into this. She had no rights left to tell him to leave now.

She bent her head. The loosened hair fell at last out of its combs and tumbled about her face, hiding her expression from him. Matt looked down at her for a moment in exasperation.

'All right,' he said at last, rising. He reached for his jacket as Katya looked up, startled. 'You win. I'll leave you to your rest and your early morning stint at the laboratory, and we'll take this down to second gear again. For the moment.'

Katya was conscious of overwhelming relief, and a faint undertow of disappointment. 'But what will you do? she blurted.

Matt gave her an ironic look. 'Don't ask, Princess. Sublimate, I guess.' He came across to her with a crooked smile and just touched her hair fleetingly as if he dared do no more. He went to the door and looked back at her. 'I'll have a bloody symphony finished in a month at this rate,' he said with hard self-mockery, before he quietly let himself out and shut the door behind him.

CHAPTER SEVEN

KATYA expected that after that there would be some constraint between them; maybe even that he would not want to see her again. It did not happen.

He met her on her doorstep the next evening with perfect equanimity, not referring to the night before. He hadn't forgotten it, of course. He made it plain he had not forgotten and he continued to remind her of it. It almost became a joke between them.

One evening he played her much of the score that he had written for *Columbus*. Katya thought it was beautiful and said so, marvelling.

'Where on earth did you find the ideas?' she asked, genuinely humbled by his talent. 'How could you *think* of these sounds?'

Matt gave her a wry look. 'Tread softly, you tread on my frustrations,' he said, and chuckled when she blushed.

He was slightly more discreet in the company of other people but only marginally so. It became a game with him: to make some reference to one of the many moments when he had felt Katya beginning to respond and then look at her wickedly under his lashes. Their companions would have no idea of their private meaning. And Katya, though she would stay outwardly calm because she had got used to the ploy, would feel a slow sweet inner clenching that, she was sure, Matt knew all about. It was another part of their secret.

He was doing it all one day when they went on a picnic in the woods. In the end, fearing that she would either blush or giggle, Katya walked away from him and began determinedly talking to other people.

There were a dozen or so people in the party,

including the nice attaché from the Embassy. He seemed glad to see Katya, even faintly curious. She thought she detected slight amusement in his face when he shook hands with her, but a cool look from Matt and a possessive hand under her elbow soon banished it.

Later, when she was sipping wine and talking, Jack came across to her. 'You look as though you're enjoying yourself,' he remarked.

She smiled. 'I am. It's perfect here.'

She raised her face to the sun filtering through green and gold leaves. He gave her an odd look.

'You're a country girl?'

She shook her head. 'No, I'm as citified as can be, I'm afraid. But like all city-dwellers I have my dreams.'

The sharp, clever face looked intrigued. 'Dreams?'

Katya gave a soft pleasurable laugh. 'Sylvan streams and leafy woods,' she told him solemnly. 'Fresh air and sunlight. The full pastoral fantasy.'

'I get you,' he nodded. 'I've seen the paintings in the Louvre too. The simple life with simple shepherds.'

And his eyes went to Matt, across the clearing, talking earnestly to another member of the party, a man who, Matt had informed Katya when they set out, built harpsichords.

Katya refused to react. She stretched, smiling. 'Yes, that's just the life for me.'

'Like Marie Antoinette? She used to play shepherdess at the Trianon, did you know that? She was a great one for pretending. Apparently they couldn't ever get her to admit that anything was serious—or dangerous. So she lost her head in the end, poor lady.'

She stared at him. What did he mean? His voice was surprisingly grave, as if they weren't talking about the poor, long-dead queen but something much nearer. Was he warning her?

Seeing the question in the puzzled violet eyes, he appeared uncomfortable. After a moment he said, 'She was quite a play-actress. She used to love dressing up and being somebody else for a time. I guess she wasn't happy with being royal—or perhaps she was ashamed of the way she behaved, sometimes.'

'You've studied Marie Antoinette?'

'I've studied people.' Jack pulled a blade of grass from between his ankles and began to peel it. 'A lot of people are like that, you know. They need a kind of holiday from themselves.'

Katya felt cold and frightened but she said calmly, 'If you're talking about Matt, I'd be glad if you were less cryptic. I'm not sure I'm following you.'

The look he gave her was both admiring and apologetic. She had the oddest feeling that he didn't like what he was doing, almost that he wasn't doing it on his own initiative.

'OK. What I'm trying to say is, if you're looking for a simple pastoral swain, you've got the wrong man in Matthew Saracen.'

It came out in a rush. Katya's brows twitched together. He *was* warning her. But why? she asked him. His smile was ironic. 'Honey, cultural attachés are an odd breed. They're not quite diplomats, not quite civil servants, and there ain't a lot of them. So they talk to each other a lot. Cultural attachés have been pulling Matt Saracen out of trouble and bailing him out of jails as long as I've been in the service.'

She stared. 'Don't you like him?'

He looked astonished. 'I love the guy. He's great. We go way back. As a friend he's terrific, as a client he's a pain, that's all. When they told me we'd got him coming to Paris, my heart sank. He's a hell-raiser.'

Katya raised her eyebrows. 'He hasn't been doing much hell-raising that I've noticed.'

Her companion was rueful. 'No, I know. That's what worries me.'

'But if he isn't giving the trouble you expected, why?'

He leaned back against her tree-stump and put his hands in the pockets of his flannels. Staring up at the sky through the branches he spoke softly, almost reluctantly.

'Because there are two ways he raises his hell. He goes off with his friends, has a few drinks, breaks up a few bars ...' He shrugged. 'Has a fight, maybe. Somebody bails him out, sobers him up, pays the fine and ships him home. Not too much damage, except to a few tables and chairs and maybe some guy with a black eye. The other way—well, to put it bluntly, the other way he finds himself a lady. Not a permanent lady, you understand, because Matt isn't into anything conventional like permanent relationships.'

Katya sat very still. Had he not told her himself only a few days ago that he did not believe in the conventions? She didn't think this man was slandering him maliciously. He was not like Dmitri, disapproving and prim. He was tolerant of Matt's ways, he liked him. But he was still saying the same things Dmitri had said.

He went on, 'And sometimes he drops out of sight. With a lady. For a while. This time it's you.' He did not look at her.

Katya said in a shaken whisper, 'Why are you telling me all this? You don't know me.'

'No, but I know about you. It's my job. And I'm told that you are alone in Paris, unprotected, that you rent a cheap room and live on a grant and what you can earn from teaching.'

She was genuinely bewildered. Did that mean that she was not a suitable escort for Matt? Surely not.

She asked, 'So?'

He gave an impatient sight, 'So if Matt lets you down, leaves you pregnant, say, I'm the one that's going to have to pick up the pieces, look after you, make sure there are no international repercussions and, if possible, that it doesn't get into the papers,' he said brutally. 'And believe me, that's a tall order. Give me the bar-smashing every time.'

Katya flinched. She felt dirty, both offended and ashamed. She wanted him to get up and leave her. She wanted never to see the clever, kindly face again.

She took a long drink, fighting for calm. At last she said, 'Thank you for your consideration,' in a satirical tone.

Again his quick look was full of admiration and, she thought, surprise. 'I'm just trying to avoid trouble, honey. You're not the type to handle it, anyone can see that. You'll get hurt.'

'And you,' she said, still cool and mocking, 'will be inconvenienced.'

He said in a flash of anger, 'If you think I'm just trying to save myself some problems, you're right. But that doesn't change the fact that it would be worse for you. I'd have difficulties with the press boys—maybe six, seven weeks. How long would it take you to get over it? Would you ever?'

She said, 'You're so sure he'll leave me?'

He gave her a look of compassion, standing up and brushing down his trousers, 'Honey, aren't you?'

The little conversation shook Katya more than she liked to admit. She found herself watching Matt for signs that his attitude to her was changing—that he was either losing interest or patience. She found neither but, in her unsettled state, did not find even that reassuring. She began to doubt her own perceptions.

So when the catastrophe finally occurred she was almost ready for it, braced as it were. Though, surprisingly, the immediate cause was not Matt Saracen but her own grandmother. Coming home from the laboratory one day, Katya was met on the doorstep of her apartment house by the grey-uniformed chauffeur of a very old and eminent Russian *emigré*, long resident in Paris. She had been introduced to him briefly at one of the Russian Club's receptions.

She paused politely, confused, as the man approached her. She knew who his master was, of course. She even wondered briefly whether Dmitri had invoked his aid in persuading her to return to his dance classes and eschew the company of unreliable American pianists.

Then, following his silent gesture, she saw who was sitting in the back of the limousine. Her heart sinking, she crossed the road and bent down to the window.

'Good evening, Grandmama,' she said with composure.

The old Princess opened the car door. Obeying the silent command, Katya got into the car and sat on the sumptuous back seat beside her. The Princess barely glanced at her.

'The Bois, Eric,' she said to the chauffeur. 'And drive on until I tell you to stop.'

He bowed and seated himself in the driving seat. As he started the engine, the Princess pressed a small button and a screen of darkened glass slipped silently into place between the chauffeur and the passenger seats.

'Now we won't be overheard,' her grandmother told Katya on a sigh.

'That's important?' Katya asked ironically.

Her grandmother for once did not look offended at this evidence of lack of proper dignity in the youngest granddaughter. Indeed, she appeared barely to notice it.

She seemed unusually hesitant. 'I am sorry to pursue you in this cloak and dagger fashion, Katerina,' she said at last. 'Your grandfather does not know I am here, and I hope he never discovers it.'

Katya stared, completely astounded. Her grandmother was a perfect, submissive wife. She never did anything without first consulting Prince Casimir, and was pained that her daughter and granddaughters had not followed her example.

Her hands, encased in three-quarter length black gloves of the softest leather, were clasped tightly on her handbag. She seemed to be under terrible strain.

'I—had to talk to you. We have been hearing——' She broke off, suddenly swinging round on Katya almost with ferocity in her mild eyes. 'Tell me, is it true that you are having an *affaire* with this man?'

Katya did not pretend not to know whom she was talking about. 'It depends on what you mean by *affaire*,' she hedged.

'Very well. Are you in love with him?'

Katya gasped. Her grandmother had never asked her such a question before. It was Prince Casimir who discussed—and at length—feelings, passions, convictions and love. His wife was the gentle, aristocratic influence who moderated the passions and led the conversation back into more decorous paths. The strongest expression of emotion she ever permitted herself or ascribed to anyone else was 'sincerely fond'. She pronounced herself so sincerely fond of her husband. And, when Vonnie was spending all her time in Antibes with a rock guitarist and getting herself into the gossip columns as a result, the Princess had said austerely that she did not believe that Vonnie was sincerely fond of her companion.

So the bald question, as much as her manner and the mysterious nature of her appearance in Paris, were all out of character for the Princess.

Katya said, 'Why do you ask?'

'Oh God,' said her grandmother, adding with this profanity yet another thing that she never did to the growing list, 'you *are* in love with him. This is horrible.'

She opened her bag with trembling fingers and

began to rummage inside. Katya watched her, feeling helpless. Eventually she produced a lace-edged handkerchief and blew her nose hard.

'You don't realise . . . you won't remember and even if you did you can't have known the *anguish* . . .' She broke off, and trumpeted into her handkerchief in a very unrestrained way. Normally she would never have permitted herself to make such an unladylike noise, thought Katya, more and more bewildered.

She leant forward and took one of her grandmother's tense hands between both of hers. 'What is it, Grandmama?' she asked gently. 'What do you want to tell me?'

The old eyes were, she found to her horror, awash with tears. The hand turned into a claw, scrabbling to cling.

'Saracen,' said the Princess with difficulty. 'Katya, you will break your heart. You will break my heart. Please, please, *please* don't see him again.'

There could be no doubting the sincerity of the plea. Katya looked at her grandmother very gravely.

'Why?' she asked at last.

The Princess closed her eyes. 'I knew you would ask that. I dreaded it.'

Katya was shaken with a sudden spurt of anger. 'And have I no right to ask it?'

There was a little silence. Then the Princess withdrew her hand from her granddaughter's and wiped her eyes. She straightened her shoulders with great dignity and, looking ahead at the back of the chauffeur's neck, said quietly, 'Yes, of course you have. Forgive me, my dear. I am upset.'

The car turned into a long boulevard. It was the rush hour, and they were momentarily becalmed in the sea of traffic.

The Princess said in a low voice, 'It was such a terrible time. I hoped it was all behind us, that it could be forgotten. But——' She turned to Katya, her expression inexpressibly sad. 'You will remember when Vonnie was eighteen, that she was ill?'

It was so completely unexpected that Katya could only stare. She did not know what she was prepared for, but she had never for a moment suspected that her grandmother had come to Paris to remind her of Vonnie's unfortunate history.

'Yes.' She failed to hide her dawning impatience.

'We said she was over-tired when anyone asked; we said she was convalescing in the country. Of course the rumour was that she had had a nervous break-down.'

'So? I'm a different temperament from Vonnie, Grandmama, and I don't have breakdowns,' Katya said.

The Princess put up a hand to shade her eyes. 'Neither did Vonnie,' she admitted quietly. She drew a long breath. 'I am afraid she was pregnant. She had a baby, Katya.' She paused again, as if enormously reluctant. 'Saracen's baby,' she concluded, not looking at her granddaughter.

Katya did not make a sound.

'She had met him at dances, she told me. When Paul was at Oxford. She used to go down to see him, he used to escort her to parties. That was where she met Saracen. He dazzled her, of course. He was so sophisticated, so worldly. And you know Vonnie—she did not stop to think, to remember her principles.'

Katya said in a voice that seemed not to be her own, 'Why didn't she marry him?'

The Princess looked shocked, more like her old self. 'Oh, that would not have done at all, of course. Vonnie herself saw that.'

'Did he——' the words were bitter as gall on her tongue, 'did he leave her then? Abandon her?'

'He saw that they were better not communicating, certainly,' the Princess said in a repressive tone, 'but he made proper provisions for the child. It would be very unfair to let you think otherwise. It is in a good home and he makes regular maintenance payments, I am told. He is very conscientious about it.'

'*Conscientious!*' It ripped out of Katya, a cry of pain and fury which she could not control.

Her grandmother jumped. 'I would not like you to misjudge him, dear. His standards may not be the same as ours, but he does have them and it would be wrong not to recognise it.'

That sounded more typical; serenely assured of where she stood and that it was the best, nay the only reasonable, position. Katya was shaken with such a fury that for the moment she hated her grandmother for that very assurance.

She turned to look blindly out at the unmoving traffic. How could he have kept it from her? The affair with Vonnie, that was bad enough, though Katya had always sensed that there was something more than simple acquaintance between him and her cousin. She had managed to persuade herself that it was dislike, though. There had always been that faint edge to his voice on the rare occasions when he mentioned Vonnie.

But a *child*! How could he pretend that the child did not exist? How could he have concealed it from her? The withholding of that information was tantamount to a grosser lie than any that Dmitri or the American diplomat had warned her against.

There was, of course, the possibility that her grandmother might be mistaken. Katya considered it, only to discard it at once. It was inconceivable that her grandmother could have been misled on such a matter. Even if Vonnie had tried to conceal the real parentage of the child, the fact that Matt had supported it over the years was proof enough that he, at least, believed he was the father. And the one thing that she was certain of, beyond any doubt, was that on a matter like that her grandmother would not lie.

She said almost to herself, 'I must see him.'

That threw her grandmother back into a flutter again, out of her dignified calm. 'Oh, no! Surely that would not be wise. It can only upset you.'

Katya's mouth stretched in a small, mirthless smile. 'You think this has not already upset me, Grandmama?'

'I'm sure it has, dear.' Her hand was taken and held comfortingly. 'I feel for you, and I admire you very deeply. You have been brave. It cannot be pleasant—but there, you always were the most independent of our grandchildren. I am afraid you will have to be very strong now, my poor child.'

Katya nodded absently. Matt was coming to the flat tonight. He had arranged to take her to a recital later, and first they were going to share a meal and a bottle of wine in her apartment. The prospect now appalled her, but it could not be avoided. And, as she had told her grandmother, she would have to see him, to say goodbye if nothing else.

Almost answering her thoughts the old Princess said coaxingly, 'Why don't you write to him, my dear? That would save you both the pain of a meeting which cannot be anything other than hurtful for you. And perhaps even for him.'

'Possibly.' Katya was not going to argue with her grandmother, or discuss it further. She felt cold with shock now that the first pain had washed over her, almost as if she were under anaesthetic. She was filled with a great calm. It was her problem and she would deal with it. There was no necessity for her grandmother to know anything more about the whole sad story.

She said, 'Would you ask the chauffeur to take me back to the apartment, please? I'd like to go home now.'

Her grandmother peered at her doubtfully. 'Are you sure? Should you be alone? I thought we might have dinner together. I am taking the ten-thirty plane back to London, but if we ate near the airport. . . .'

Katya shook her head decisively. 'No.' That sounded brutal. She managed a conciliatory smile that seemed to come from a long way away. 'I'm sorry, I have to think.'

'Of course, dear.' At once her grandmother was all understanding, but persistent. 'And you won't do anything silly like run straight to that man as soon as I've gone?'

'I won't run to him,' Katya promised steadily, omitting to mention that there was no need to do so. He would probably be waiting for her on her return.

The Princess sighed. 'You're a good girl underneath. I have always said you would never do anything— *wrong*. Though I suppose all young people have to rebel. When you are my age, you will know what really matters: dignity, honour, self-respect.'

'Kindness?' asked Katya quietly. She found her grandmother's rapid transition back to her usual gentle self-satisfaction unpleasing.

'Well, of course, dear.' The wide violet eyes which had once been the talk of the Russian capital and were a legacy to her granddaughter were full of reproach. 'We never treated you with anything other than kindness at home. You cannot say we did.'

Katya shrugged. 'And it came a long way after a sense of family dignity. Perhaps if it hadn't, poor Vonnie wouldn't have been so reckless.'

'Katya!' It was a shocked reproof. 'We cannot escape what we are, what we owe to our forefathers and to those who come after us.'

Katya gave a twisted smile. 'So I have often heard grandfather say. I think it is meretricious snobbery and I reject it. Now, are you going to ask the chauffeur to take me back or shall I get out and walk to the Métro?'

In great offence the Princess leaned forward and

rapped on the glass. When the chauffeur answered on the intercom she gave the necessary order in a curt voice. She sat back in her seat, not looking at Katya.

The silence was broken only once in the ride back to Katya's flat. That was when the Princess said haughtily, 'You do not need me to tell you your duty. You know it well enough. And I will not be blamed for the difficulties that you young girls get into through your own blind wilfulness. If you had stayed at home where your place was and married young Simon, none of this would have happened.'

Katya swung round on her, eyes flashing. 'Vonnie would still have had her child,' she hissed.

The Princess, for all her self-righteousness, quailed. She made no attempt to answer and almost at once Katya turned her back, looking out into the roads they passed without really seeing them. When they reached the front of her apartment building she alighted at once, without waiting for the chauffeur to get out of his cab and come and open the door for her.

'Goodbye, Grandmama,' she said distantly. 'I may write. Until I do, please don't try to get in touch with me again. Or,' she added, reflecting that if her grandmother had her address in Paris in spite of all the subterfuge, it was very possible that Prince Casimir had also discovered it, 'let my grandfather do so.'

She strode away without looking back, not even turning when she heard the great car glide away.

Katya went up the uncarpeted steps in a dream. She didn't know whether she was more afraid of finding Matt in her room waiting for her or of having to sit there in solitude, agonising over what she should eventually say to him. It was an unimportant problem which occupied her totally, so that when she opened the door and found him sitting on her fireside chair with his heels on the fender, she jumped in genuine surprise.

He had been reading a journal. He raised his head as soon as she came in, dropping it lightly to the floor. The faint squashy sound it made showed that it was quite a bulky thing; probably one of his musical journals, she thought. They were always very bulky. By concentrating hard on the bulkiness of musical papers she was managing to block out the sudden atrocious pain of seeing him, so friendly and comfortable and welcoming.

Matt stretched and grinned at her. 'You're late. I was beginning to nod off.'

So her face did not show the terrible wound she had just been dealt. Well, that wasn't surprising really, thought Katya with cynicism. His face did not show the treachery he had been guilty of every hour, every day since he first came up to her at that reception.

She said woodenly, 'I'm sorry. I was held up.'

Something in her tone must have alerted him. His eyes narrowed and, suddenly, she saw his face change. He came to his feet in a lithe movement, apparently all concern.

'What's the matter?'

She turned away from that deceiving, concerned face, unbuttoning her coat.

'Did I say anything was the matter?'

'You didn't have to. You look like death. What is it? Something at work? Something you saw on the way home?'

She shook her head, suddenly unable to speak for the tears that clogged her throat. He took the coat from her cold fingers and made as if to take her in his arms.

'Have a cuddle and tell me about it,' he invited, his voice warm and teasing.

'*No!*' It was a single vicious syllable. His arms fell to his side as if he had been struck. Katya turned aside.

He said slowly, 'You're badly shaken. I've never seen you like this. What *is* it?'

With her back to him, Katya said in an unrecognisable voice, 'Matt, will you answer me one question and tell me the truth?'

He went very still.

'Will you?' she persisted.

'I have always told you the truth,' Matt said in a still voice.

She gave a little laugh. It was an ugly sound. 'In your fashion.'

'I have never lied to you.' He sounded angry.

'Then don't lie to me now.' She swung round on him, suddenly desperate. 'They tell me that Vonnie has a child and you support it: is that true?'

The grey eyes flared and then went utterly and disconcertingly blank.

'Is it?'

In the last unnerving silence that followed Katya felt as if she were only being kept on her feet by the tension, almost palpable, that hummed between them. She had the illusion that when he released her from his laser glance, she would subside on the floor as limp as yesterday's washing.

'More or less,' he drawled at last.

Katya gave a little animal cry of pain that she could not have suppressed to save her life and whirled, turning her back on him as she pressed both fists against her shaking mouth.

He did not attempt to touch her.

'You shouldn't listen to gossip,' he said contemptuously.

Katya was shivering so hard that she could not stop. She felt light-headed. Matt was clearly unmoved by her distress, watching her without speaking. Eventually she sank down into the chair he had vacated, reaching out a hand that shook like an old woman's to turn on the fire.

He moved, sitting down opposite her. He looked at her levelly.

'Someone has obviously been spilling poison into your ears. You'd better tell me who.' He was, she thought incredulously, completely unrepentant, even caustic: it was as if she, not he, were to blame.

Her throat moved. 'My grandmother.'

That startled him, she heard it in his indrawn breath. She looked up, miserably triumphant.

'Are you going to try and tell me that my grandmother came over to Paris to slander you gratuitously?' she asked.

'No, I——'

'Because she's not a gossip and she does not spread poison,' said Katya pugnaciously sweeping over his reply.

'No, I realise that. I hadn't, that is I thought—oh hell, I suppose I thought Jack or someone like that had been getting at you and you just hadn't been loyal enough to ask me for my side before you judged and condemned me.' Matt sounded really shaken. 'I'm sorry, love, honestly.'

He reached out a hand, which she ignored.

'But if it had been Jack rather than my grandmother, it would still have been true, wouldn't it? Whether I'd been poor fool enough to be loyal, as you put it, or not. It would still have been true.'

She lifted her eyes briefly, hating him. Matt's face was bleak. His hand dropped.

'What is truth?'

'What I just asked you for,' Katya flashed. 'When you said that what my grandmother told me was true. Oh, I'm sorry,' she mimicked him, 'more or less true.'

'I should have said that your grandmother wasn't lying. She told you the facts as she understood them.' He leaned forward suddenly; Katya saw that he was very pale. 'But you know facts aren't always what they seem, they can be selected. And truth,' his voice was bitter, 'is rarely self-evident.'

Her heart was pounding hard and she felt very cold. She shrank a little in her chair away from him. She felt that he was about to reach out and take her hand and flinched from the thought of that contact.

'All right,' her voice was deceptively mild, 'I've heard my grandmother's facts, selected or not. I'm in no position to judge that, of course. Now you tell me your facts.'

She hardly sounded encouraging, and Matt clearly recognised it. When she flickered a glance at his face she found it set and grim. At last she could bear the unnerving silence no longer.

'Is it true that you paid Vonnie's bills?' she shot at him.

Matt was disconcerted. For a moment, before the mask descended again, she could sense how completely unexpected the question was to him.

Then his mouth twisted. 'You have a genius for asking the wrong questions.'

'Wrong from whose point of view?' Katya countered. '*Did* you?'

'I——' He paused and, with a startlingly savage gesture said, 'Oh hell, yes, I did.'

She tipped her head back against the wing of the chair, staring at the ceiling. If she kept her eyes wide and concentrated hard she would be able to repress the welling tears. She expelled a long breath.

'And in spite of that you—sought my company? Took me out? Knowing I—knew nothing?'

Matt's face was unreadable. 'Yes.'

'You let me—trust you. When you knew it was all a lie.'

'You have never trusted me,' he said in a remote voice. 'That's been plain from the first.'

Katya shivered. 'I know,' she said miserably, half ashamed of it. Then she shook her hair back in defiance and glared at him. 'And I wasn't wrong, was I? Oh, I got the *specifics* wrong. I thought it was Steffy Solomon you were really interested in. . . .'

Matt interrupted in a deadly voice. 'Are you suggesting that I am *really interested*, as you put it, in your appalling cousin?'

'Don't talk about her like that,' flashed Katya. 'You're in no position to criticise.'

There was a tense pause. Then he said, 'Hell!' explosively and flung himself away to look out of the window, one hand running distractedly through his hair.

At last he said, 'Will you let me tell you about it?'

That hurt, searing her feelings like a brand.

'No!' she almost shouted. It was pure instinct talking. She began to shiver. 'I don't want to know anything about it. I can imagine sufficient.' Her mouth twisted painfully. 'I can imagine too much for my own good.'

He turned at that and took a quick step towards her. 'Ah, darling, don't . . .' he said in a voice that seemed to have been wrenched out of him. 'Don't hurt yourself like this.'

She gave him a level look. 'I think the hurt has already been done. And not by me.'

Matt flinched. 'All right, I should have told you. I know. I knew all along. But, don't you see? I didn't dare.'

Katya turned her face away. 'Yes, I see,' she said dully.

'You were so shy, so cautious. I had to go so carefully to win your confidence . . .'

'Did it seem to you that you deserved my confidence?' she asked in a polite voice.

He did not look ashamed. 'Yes,' he told her evenly. 'Yes, it did. Apart from this one thing, which happened a long time ago and has nothing to do with you and me, I was absolutely straight with you. I told you things I have told no one else. Things I had, up till then, barely admitted to myself.'

She ignored the last part of what he said. 'Nothing to do with you and me?' she echoed disbelievingly. 'How can you say that? When you have a *child*!' It was a cry of anguish.

Matt's face twisted. 'Will you *listen* to me for a moment? Forget what your grandmother said.'

'How can I?' Katya asked sadly. 'When you tell me that there *is* a child.'

'Yes, but it isn't as it looks. I can't tell you everything. I can't really tell you anything now, without asking . . . Oh, damn, Katya, can't you trust me, just for a little?'

She stood up. 'I tried,' she said. 'I really tried. For a while I did trust you. And my grandmother has just shown me how wrong I was. You've been telling me what a bad influence my grandparents are, Matt, but at least they have always told me the truth. They haven't tried to keep me in some fool's paradise while they manipulated me.' Her voice broke.

Matt was white about the mouth; she suddenly realised that he was very angry. When he spoke, it was hardly above a whisper; and it was vicious.

'You're sure of that?' His laugh was mocking. 'You trust them? You know what they're like, you know what they've done to yourself and your cousin, but you'd still rather trust them than me?'

'They haven't lied to me,' she said bitingly.

'There are lies and lies, as you'll find out one day, Princess.'

'Not from you,' she said in swift repudiation. 'Never from you.'

'Oh yes, possibly even from a weak and sinning mortal like me. If you can ever bring yourself to admit that Grandmother was wrong, that is.' He drew a long breath. 'God, you sit there, as prim as you please, and lecture me on things that happened ten years ago that you know nothing about! And all because that dear, sweet old lady your grandmother has told you what to think. Without so much as the formality of a speech for the defence, I am accused and condemned in one go over the teacups. Well, fine, if that's the way you want it. It's a shame because we had a lot going for us. Or we would have had, if you'd been a living, breathing woman and not Grandmother's puppet. The laugh is on me in the end for thinking there was a real woman under that exquisite face of yours.'

He took a hasty step towards her. It was so unexpected that Katya didn't have time to avoid him. He took her face between his hands, stared down at it for a moment as if he barely recognised her, and then his mouth closed on hers in a kiss of such cold force that she felt faint. It was an insult. It was meant to be an insult. Something shrivelled inside her.

Then Matt released her, putting her away from him as if she were an instrument he had tried and found unsatisfactory. His face was very white and his eyes were blazing, but when he spoke it was in a light, lazy voice of extreme insolence.

'Spare me the maidenly reproaches. I won't touch you again.'

And, before she could think of anything to say, he left.

CHAPTER EIGHT

KATYA did not see him again. She did not expect to.

She threw herself into her work, staying till all hours in the science building, long after the day's work in the laboratory was over. The Programme Director asked her to help him with some lectures that he was giving, an additional burden of work that she welcomed. She took more classes herself. She was always willing to fill in for other people when they were called away or fell ill. With a little careful management, in fact, she contrived to reduce her hours in her own apartment to the bare minimum necessary for sleep.

The weekends were bad, though. Sometimes she would come into the science building and use the library, but even that was shut on Sundays. So she would pack up a small lunch, which she subsequently forgot to eat, and take the Métro to the far end of the line. When she reached her destination, she would simply get out and walk until it was time to turn round and walk back. It was excellent exercise and she must have seen some interesting landscapes—she could never afterwards remember where she had been or what she had seen. She walked in a methodical, determined way, her eyes blankly noting landmarks to aid the return journey and dismissing them from her memory the moment they had served their purpose. They were chill little excursions and, as the days grew shorter and the weather bleaker, they became more so.

Babette, noticing the look of exhaustion on Katya's face, took her to task.

'You are not happy, one can see that. But that is no excuse for working yourself into the ground,' she scolded.

It was lunchtime. They were sitting facing each other in a small café much patronised by students and Katya was stirring a plate of excellent râgout with her fork in pitiful pretence of eating.

She said, 'I enjoy my work.'

'My child, at the moment you do not look as if you enjoy anything,' Babette told her frankly.

Katya shrugged. 'I find it satisfying. My work is going very well, and the Professor . . .'

She was ruthlessly interrupted. 'The Professor is making shameless use of you, as you well know. And even *he* is beginning to have a conscience about it. He told Henri, in my hearing, that you have more or less prepared his notes for the Geneva lectures.'

Again Katya lifted her shoulders. 'I was interested.'

'Naturally. It is your subject. And you have already finished your thesis, so you might just as well make use of your time that way as any other,' agreed Babette in a casual tone.

'Exactly. There's no point in . . .' Katya broke off. 'Who told you I'd finished my thesis?'

Babette leaned forward, smiling. 'Nobody. I guessed. Henri has a pretty strong suspicion, too. It was a little trap of mine to make you admit it.'

Katya looked away, trying not to be angry at the way she had been caught out. Babette meant it for the best, she knew.

Now the French girl was saying soberly, 'And it is not just because the programme was going well. Not even because of the Professor's Swiss lectures, was it? You finish your thesis twelve months before it is due to be submitted for no other reason than that you have not been doing anything else for weeks.' She paused. 'Not since you stopped seeing this man, whoever he is.'

Katya's head jerked round, her eyes unguarded and, in that startled moment, full of anguish. Babette's lively face softened.

'Oh, poor Katya! Is it so bad?'

Katya dragged the remnants of her composure together and gave the matter her consideration.

'I don't suppose so, no. Not compared with the things that other people have to contend with, anyway.'

Babette was not impressed. 'So why do you wander about looking like a child locked out of Paradise?' she demanded.

Katya was faintly annoyed. 'I don't.'

'Oh yes, you do,' Babette said firmly. 'Whenever you think people aren't looking at you, you forget to smile. And one can see that you are in a tragedy,' she assured her solemnly.

Katya said in a deprecating tone, 'Then my looks belie me,' and when Babette looked disbelievingly said a little desperately, 'Honestly, Babette, it's not a tragedy. I dare say it's very ordinary—a love affair that went wrong, that's all. The same thing probably happened to thousands of girls all over Paris this summer.'

'Thousands of girls in Paris are not off their food and working sweat-shop hours,' Babette observed neutrally. 'Nor looking as if they haven't slept for a month.'

Katya shifted in her seat. 'Yes, well. I'm willing to admit I haven't been very philosophical about it. It was the first time, you see. The first time I'd been in love.'

There, she thought. *I've said it! I've said it out loud and it still sounds true.*

Babette was watching her cautiously. She expressed neither surprise at Katya's announcement nor disbelief that she had not been in love before. Nor was there any pity apparent on her face, though she looked thoughtful.

'It must have happened very quickly,' she remarked. 'You decided you were in love and you parted all in the space of three or four weeks.'

Katya bit her lip. 'Not quite.'

'No? You had known him before?'

Katya shook her head. 'Not that, no. But I didn't realise that, well, that I was in love with him,' she said in a rush. 'Not until he'd gone.'

There was considerable understanding in the older woman's eyes.

'It happens so often, *chérie*. We women are like that. Who is this man who is always on our doorstep? We can summon him whenever we went. Pouf, we cannot be bothered.' She waved a dismissive hand at an imaginary suitor. She sighed. 'But then he leaves the doorstep and we realise how very necessary it is that he should be there. Sometimes,' she added on a more practical note, 'that is why they take themselves off. They are not entirely fools. Is it possible that this man of yours is teaching you a lesson?'

'No,' said Katya desolately, with absolute conviction.

Babette was not convinced. 'Have you telephoned him? Written to him?'

'No.'

'Or could you bump into him by accident? It can be very helpful and is not usually difficult to arrange,' Babette suggested.

Katya smiled but said again, 'No.'

Her friend looked disapproving. 'You are not willing to meet him halfway? Not when you are breaking your heart for him? she demanded, shocked at this cowardice, to say nothing of the lack of enterprise in her friend.

Katya finally pushed away her plate in a spurt of disgust and stopped pretending that she could eat anything.

'I can't,' she said in a suffocated voice. 'And I can't talk about it any more. *Please*, Babette.'

'*Eh bien!*' Babette shrugged, not quite offended but nevertheless displeased. 'You know your own business best,' she observed in a tone which made it clear that she thought exactly the opposite. 'I will not mention the matter again.'

Nor did she, though it was perfectly obvious to Katya that there were times when Babette had an almost physical struggle to restrain herself. Katya meanwhile did her best to put all thoughts of Matt Saracen out of her head. She never thought about those few magical weeks, never referred to them in conversation or her letters home and she never, under any circumstances, mentioned his name.

She did not, however, manage to go back to the life she had led before she met him. For one thing she could no longer bear to see Dmitri Kolkanin. He telephoned her a couple of times and she even met him by chance at a friend's house. On each occasion she got away as soon as she could, hoping that her burning resentment did not show. It was not made easier by the fact that the resentment was mingled with shame. Dmitri, after all, was one of the few people to be in a position to guess exactly what it was that had happened to her in that empty summer city.

Katya stopped pretending to her grandparents too: the elaborate postal arrangements were discontinued. She stopped writing them the long chatty letters, as well. It had been a struggle to write at all but in the end she had done it, more from a sense of pride than anything else. She was not going to permit herself to be so feeble that she was afraid of the influence of her grandparents any longer, she told herself.

She had written, therefore, saying that she was well, she was working hard, she would keep in touch but she did not want to see them. They had taken it surprisingly well. Her grandfather telephoned her once, at work, and she cut him off short, saying quietly that she did not want to talk. He had not tried again.

The Princess had, predictably, apparently decided to ignore the whole thing now that she had got her way. Undeterred by Katya's curtness, she wrote long letters detailing the fortunes of Paul and his wife and son, even—with what Katya found unbelievable blandness—Vonnie. She wrote at length about the important things in her life—clothes and the decoration of the flat, Prince Casimir's old friends—and asked not one word about Katya's life.

So much bland insensitivity infuriated Katya. Her grandmother could not be under any illusion about the effect her announcement had had on Katya. She had been shattered, horrified and full of grief. Her grandmother knew her too well not to have recognised something at least of what she had felt. Yet now she was going to put it all behind them; she would make believe that Katya's life in Paris was busy and fufilled. The personal tragedy which she had, in her own way, helped to bring about was in the Princess's eyes now over. And when such things were over they were best ignored.

Her affectionate, complacent letters were the only thing that autumn that managed to rouse Katya from her emotional apathy. Otherwise she felt as if she were in limbo. She worked with passion, utterly dedicated to the project, but people barely invaded her consciousness. They were like shadows on the edge of a dream. She knew they were there but they did not matter. All that mattered was her laboratory, her graphs and her computer.

There is no telling how long she would have gone on in this way had it not been for the advent of Christmas, and two incidents that roused her to some awareness of her surroundings. The first was a brief exchange with the Professor, whom she met on the steps of the chemistry building one lunchtime.

'Katya,' he beamed, proud of knowing the Christian name of his most conscientious researcher, 'that Swiss lecture. Very well received, they tell me. I'm going back to a symposium in the middle of December.

Think you ought to come this time, join in the discussions.'

Katya was startled. He did not normally travel with members of his staff. His next words explained it.

'Going to be a lot of the younger men there. Technical problems being aired.' The Professor, though distinguished and highly intellectual, was largely uninterested in the techniques used for getting his widely publicised results. He would want one of his assistants to talk about the experimental difficulties they had encountered, and Henri's wife was expecting a baby, which would make Henri unavailable.

'It sounds interesting,' she commented, which was true. 'I'm flattered that you should ask me.' Which was not.

He smiled and nodded, not noticing the irony, and proceeded into the building in his usual stately manner.

At first Katya thought that she would go with him to Geneva and then fly straight back to England for the enormous family Christmas that was celebrated every year. She had not thought about going home, she had just assumed that she would do so. Then the second incident occurred and she changed her mind.

She was shopping for a warm sweater, wandering indifferently between shelves of bright woollen garments, when she heard her name called.

'Katerina! Katya! It *is* you.'

She turned to see her cousin Paul, his large face wreathed in smiles, surging towards her. She held out both hands to him in sudden and unfeigned pleasure.

'Paul, how good to see you. But what are you doing here?'

He shrugged. 'Oh, work, nothing exciting. I'm here setting up a contract. But you——' He took her by the shoulders and held her away from him. 'You're supposed to be in some academic fastness, or that's what the grandparents told me.' He grinned suddenly. 'Was it one of Grandmama's polite fictions, then?'

Katya shook her head, slipping her hand through his arm. 'No. I'm at the university here.'

'Oho!' He covered her small cold hand with his own. 'Sounds like a good compromise. Come and tell me all about it.'

'But your contract . . .?'

'In the hands of the typists even as we speak. I've ventured out with a shopping list as long as your arm that Anna pressed into my hand just as I was leaving for the airport.' He pulled a face; he was very fond of his wife and always did what she asked, but he was not a man who enjoyed crowded shops. 'She keeps a permanent list of stuff she wants from Paris for when Vonnie comes over, only this time I've drawn the short straw.'

Katya's smile became a little fixed. 'Vonnie keeping away from Paris these days?'

Paul shot her a quick, shrewd look. 'Vonnie seems settled in the States for the moment,' he said. 'Says New York agrees with her. She's even got some sort of job, I think.'

'I can't imagine that,' Katya said, making an effort to sound normal.

'No, it doesn't sound likely. I expect there's a man involved,' he said indifferently. 'Not that Grandmama would admit it.'

Her smile was a mere stretch of the lips, he saw with concern. He conducted her to the door of the apartment store and guided her to one of the pavement cafés, talking lightly all the time. It was too cold to sit outside, even under cover, so he led the way into the interior of the café and ordered steaming coffee. He stowed his purchases under the tubular steel chair with a grunt and smiled at her.

'Now tell me why you look ready to spit,' he invited. 'The grandparents been getting at you?'

'You could put it like that.'

'What about?'

Their coffee arrived and she sipped it defensively. 'What is it usually about?' she said with bitterness.

Paul thought for a moment. 'Career. Marriage. Dignity.' He quirked an eyebrow. 'That's what immediately leaps to mind.'

Katya smiled reluctantly. 'None of those.'

'No?' He was frowning. 'What, then? Unless you're following in Vonnie's footsteps and chasing rock guitarists,' he teased.

One look at her face and the laughter was wiped off his own. For a moment the kind eyes were shocked. Then he leaned forward.

'My stupid tongue,' he said remorsefully. 'I'm sorry, Katoushka, I didn't think.' He put out a hand. Silently she put her own into it and was grateful for the warm fingers that closed comfortingly round it. 'Do you want to talk about him?'

'Him?' she hedged.

'Your rock guitarist,' he said, but gently. 'Or equivalent.'

She shifted sharply as if struck by a sudden pain. 'Wrong instrument. Otherwise——' She broke off, shrugging.

Paul looked puzzled. 'You've fallen for a musician? That doesn't sound like you. A teacher, maybe, or one of your dedicated scientist types——'

'You're wrong. I'm more like Vonnie than any of you guessed,' Katya said with cool self-mockery. 'I've fallen for the conventional disastrous man. Not only a musician but unreliable, untruthful and with an appalling past.'

Paul did not laugh. Neither did he look particularly shocked. He surveyed her calmly, taking in the bitter line of the beautiful mouth and the shadowed eyes and remarked, 'And what sort of future?'

'What?' Katya almost jumped, the question was so unexpected.

'Future,' he explained patiently. 'Not by any means

the same as the past. Especially if he now has my most beautiful cousin in love with him.'

Katya's laugh cracked. 'He had your *most* beautiful cousin several years ago, I gather,' she said.

Paul sat bolt upright at that, looking disturbed at last. 'What the hell are you talking about?'

Katya averted her eyes which had a tendency to fill with tears when she let down her guard. She said carefully, with no expression whatsoever in her voice, 'My luck was out. I happened to chance on one of Vonnie's cast-offs, that's all.'

Paul was quite simply disbelieving. 'Dear girl, that has to be nonsense! You and Vonnie wouldn't even look at the same man. If she says any different, she's just being mischievous.' He frowned, concerned. 'Though I agree that's not like her.'

'No, Vonnie's no mischief-maker,' said Katya. 'And she hasn't said a word, Paul, honestly. It was Grandmama.'

'*What?*'

'And she's not a mischief-maker either.'

'*Grandmama?* Grandmama told you about one of Vonnie's men? Grandmama, who doesn't admit they exist when they're around, still less when they've been discarded? Kitten, you are having hallucinations,' Paul said kindly.

In spite of herself she was moved to laughter but was soon sober again, the violet eyes sad.

'No, I'm afraid not, Paul. She even came to Paris to tell me about it.'

He stared at her. Behind the large, clever face the brain was clearly working fast, sifting what she had said and drawing his own conclusions. At last he said in the sort of unemotional voice he must use on overwrought clients, Katya thought, 'What instrument?'

Again she jumped, disconcerted. 'The piano,' she responded at once, without thinking.

His face changed. He shut his eyes, and Katya drank coffee, grateful for its warmth. She was very cold. Her fingers' ends, she saw with remote interest, were blue and her hands were shaking slightly.

'Are you telling me that you are in love with Matthew Saracen?' Paul asked at last.

Katya did not answer. She was confused though, she discovered, not really surprised by his powers of deduction. Paul was the cleverest of her cousins and more than capable of using that intelligence to get to the heart of a mystery. No, it was not Matt's identity that gave her pause but Paul's invitation to her to say that she was in love with him. She was not going to admit that to anyone within the family, not even as kind and concerned a cousin as Paul.

She said, to deflect him, 'Do you know him, then?'

Paul looked haggard. 'God help me, I introduced them. We were at Oxford together. And then his father took that house at Yarnton and we used to have parties there. But——' He broke off. 'Did Grandmama *say* he was one of Vonnie's cast-offs, Katya?'

She swallowed. It still hurt to think about that. He watched her pinched face and swore. It was so unusual in gentle Paul that Katya was startled, her eyes flying to his face in startled question.

'Don't bother to answer that,' he said grimly. 'May God preserve me from morally upright grandmothers! What is as deadly as a self-righteous woman?'

'She—she thought I ought to know,' Katya said in a strained voice that was little more than a whisper.

'I'm sure she did.'

Katya's shoulders drooped. 'And she was right, in a way, because M-Matt,' she stumbled over his name, 'hadn't said a word about it. Left to himself he wouldn't have mentioned it. And it was hardly—unimportant.'

Paul was looking troubled. 'So the only version you've heard is Grandmama's?' He touched her soft dark hair compassionately. 'Look, pet, no matter what her motives—and I don't for a moment think they were disinterested—Grandmama can't know the whole truth of what went on all those years ago. Talk it over with Matt. Don't accuse him. Just ask him for the truth.'

'I did.' She looked away. 'He said Grandmama was right.'

'Oh, Katya,' sighed Paul. 'You must have made him furious.'

She looked faintly surprised. 'How did you guess? Surely it was *me* who should have been furious? He'd lied to me. Anyway, I—can't ask him anything any more because I haven't seen him, and I don't know where he is. It's over, Paul.'

He looked at her very gravely. 'Is it? When you've got shadows like that under your eyes? You're not a fool, Katoushka, and you used not to be a coward. Don't lie to yourself.'

She said in a low, intense voice, 'It has to be over. I couldn't live with knowing—I *couldn't*.'

Paul said with sudden resolution, 'Look, Katya, just because Grandmama is a dear sweet old lady, it doesn't also mean that she isn't a calculating old bag who twists the truth to suit herself. Go and see Vonnie, if you won't talk to Matt. You know Vonnie. She may be wild and woolly, but she's honest and she won't spin you a tale like Grandmama.'

Katya flinched from the very thought. 'No!'

'But——'

'No. It couldn't make any difference. Even if . . . *He* doesn't want me any more,' she said with terrible simplicity. 'That's the point, Paul. Even if I could do—what you suggest—even if I changed my mind; it wouldn't make any difference. Matt Saracen has had enough of me, and that's the end of the matter.'

He reached for her hands again, saying no more. She gave him a tremulous smile.

'Poor little Katya. What a mess,' he said sadly. 'Who'd have a family?'

She nodded, not speaking. They finished their coffee in silence and then he went back to finish his shopping. He was still kind, but a constraint had entered their meeting. It left Katya feeling tense and on the edge of tears, which dismayed her.

It was after that she decided she could not go home for Christmas. She could not face her grandparents' curiosity and well-intentioned bullying, but, worse than that, she could not face Paul's kindness. It would sweep away the last of her defences and plunge her back into that hell of self-pity which she had made such determined efforts to struggle out of.

Her decision was greeted with resignation by her grandparents, it seemed. The Princess wrote her a letter of carefully worded reproach but her grandfather, unexpectedly tactful, sent her a cheque 'To enjoy herself in Geneva'. She told the Professor that she would not only accompany him but stay on after his departure for the whole of the festive season, and a room in a lakeside hotel was booked for her.

It was the oddest Christmas of her life. She had never spent it away from home before, nor had there ever been a Christmas when she was not surrounded by family and friends exchanging good wishes and hopes for the New Year. It made her feel oddly unlike herself to be in a hotel which, though festive enough, was inhabited only by strangers. Katya felt very alone.

It was, however, solitude of her own choosing. There had been several delegates at the conference whose homes were in Geneva all the year round and who had invited her to their houses for some part of the festival. She had refused them all.

Katya was not quite clear why she felt it so necessary to be alone. Babette had said roundly that it was unhealthy, and perhaps she was right; Katya could not help herself, though. Other people felt like intruders.

Her meeting with Paul had brought back Matt and the memory of their hours together with terrifying vividness. She began to dream about him; to dream not just of the things they had done and seen together, but of whole new areas that she had never shared with Matt but felt, somehow, as if she should have done. The cruellest of all of these was when she would wake up, cold in the early morning, and reach for him out of a bone-deep conviction that he would be in bed beside her. It did no good to remind herself that they had never shared a bed, and that that was mainly by her choice. She felt as if they had belonged together in every sense and that she was now in mourning for him.

It was unsettling. In Paris she would leap out of bed, shivering, and switch on her fire before flinging herself into work. In Geneva there was no therapeutic early-morning task but she could, and did, take herself out for extended walks among the pines.

It was there, on the mountain path one morning, that she met a man strolling down the snowy path towards her. She hesitated in surprise. At that hour she was usually the only walker about. He smiled and raised his hat. He looked almost, she thought in half suspicion, as if he had expected to see her; even come out for the purpose of meeting her.

But he did not speak. Having raised his hat he simply passed her on the wide path, continuing down in the direction of the lake and the hotel. Katya shrugged and put him out of her mind.

He was recalled only that evening. She was sitting at her usual table on her own in the heavily curtained window embrasure when she looked up and saw him come into the dining room. He was not on his own this time; he had a boy with him, quite a sturdy child but not more than nine or ten, Katya thought, wondering about their relationship. Perhaps he was the child's grandfather? If so, he seemed a good deal more relaxed about it than Prince Casimir had ever been. He was talking to the boy as if they were equals, sharing laughter, and the child plainly adored him. For the first time in that strange holiday Katya felt a pang of real loneliness.

She was startled out of it by the appearance at her elbow of an apologetic waiter.

Would Mademoiselle André mind, on just this one occasion, sharing her table? The hotel was expecting a party, there had been a small error, there was no table free. Katya frowned and he redoubled his excuses: it would be of great assitance to the hotel and there would, of course, be a suitable reduction in the bill if she would be so gracious as to agree. And Mr Alexander, as she could see, was a gentleman who would not annoy her in any way while the boy was exquisitely mannered. And, being American, their native language was English and Mademoiselle would be able to speak her own tongue again.

Mademoiselle abandoned resistance, since it was clearly hopeless, with a faint shrug. The waiter looked across at the man and boy with a nod. They approached and sat down.

'Hello, there. We met on the path this morning,' the man said, smiling. 'I'm Stacy Alexander, and this is Tom.'

The boy said hello politely, wide eyes considering her. He was a very self-possessed ten-year-old, Katya decided, until he looked at his companion for guidance. Stacy Alexander smiled down at him reassuringly.

Katya murmured a greeting.

'Are you staying in this hotel?' he asked chattily.

'Yes.' She realised more was expected of her. 'Are you?'

'Not so far—we might.' He looked at the boy. 'How do you feel about it, Tom? Do you like it here?'

The boy gave a sudden grin, revealing uneven teeth and a childish dimple. 'Sure, if it means we stop moving around.'

Stacy Alexander sighed, turning to Katya. 'I thought he'd have a wonderful holiday in Europe, but all he does is complain about the travelling,' he said, teasing the boy.

Katya smiled at Tom. 'Would you rather spend Christmas at home, then?'

He shook his head decisively. 'Nope! I want to spend Christmas with Stacy. If he wants to jump planes all over Europe,' he added with adult mockery, 'that's OK too.'

'You like Geneva,' Stacy protested. 'You can ski . . .'

'Sure. I can ski at home too,' said the boy reasonably.

'And it'll be good for your French.'

'Sure,' said Tom again. He encompassed Katya in a solemn look. 'You want to talk French, Miss André?'

'*Tom!*' It was a rebuke. Katya could sense that, though it was said lightly, it was nevertheless a real one. There was an undercurrent here that she couldn't quite make out, but which made her uneasy. Though she liked them both, she thought, at least on first acquaintance. Perhaps she should probe a little.

'Forgive me,' she said to Stacy Alexander, 'but do we know each other? I had the oddest feeling on the path this morning that we had met.'

He smiled, very relaxed. 'No, I don't think we've ever met, Miss André, though you may have seen me on the screen. I'm an old hack actor, I'm afraid, with too many bad movies to my credit to want to admit. A lot of people think they've met me before, though.'

'I see.' She did not, and she was almost sure that it was not that but she could not say as much since he categorically denied knowing her and she couldn't remember where she thought they had met. 'I'm sorry.'

'Don't be.' This time his smile was as wide and charming as Tom's, and equally full of mockery. 'It's good to know the face is not forgotten, even if you can't put a name on it.'

She raised her brows. 'Not Stacy Alexander, then?'

He and the boy exchanged a look of pleasurable conspiracy. 'Not Stacy Alexander,' he agreed.

On that one point he remained mysterious, but on everything else he was frankness itself. He made no secret of the fact that he liked Katya and was glad he had met her. Before the end of the evening she found herself invited to go skating with them the next morning and, slightly to her own surprise, accepted.

They were staying in a much larger and altogether grander hotel than her own, a little further along the lake. Stacy Alexander had a luxurious suite overlooking the water where Tom welcomed her when she arrived at eleven.

'Stacy's talking Transatlantic,' he informed her, 'and I've got to go and buy him some film. He left all of his in Paris. He said to make yourself at home, coffee's coming.'

Katya smiled as the boy clattered off down the corridor. She went to the window with its peaceful picture-postcard scene. The hotel was modern, with radiators neatly disguised under the banquette that was set in the window embrasure. The seat was covered in bright patchwork cushion dinted where the boy had been sitting, and the magazines he had been reading were littered about the floor.

Katya bent to tidy them. They were largely English language though there were a couple of French publications, none of them for children. She was just wondering a little at his unchildlike taste when her eye fell on an article on one of the open pages.

'*Triumph of American Pianist*,' she read and beside it, not really recognisable, was a photograph of Matt making him look dark-browed and bad tempered. Her heart fell like a stone and she sat limply on the window seat. She could no more have put down the magazine than she could have remained on her feet.

'Matthew Saracen, the former Westminster prize winner, received a standing ovation in Chicago tonight,' it said, going on to describe the triumphal concert in hyperbolic detail. The journalist had clearly been moved to enthusiasm by the performance but could not quite disguise the slight hint of surprise. That he had not expected Saracen to give a performance of Brahms's masterpiece that was as powerful as this, was clearly what he meant and did not say. Remembering the equivocal tone of the earlier reviews she had read, Katya tried hard to be glad.

She looked at the date. It was less than a month ago. Well, she had never expected that Matt would cease playing the piano because of the end of their affair; it was his livelihood, after all. And if she was resentful that he had been so unaffected by the sort of feelings that beset her that he was playing better than ever, well, that was because she was silly, trivial and emotional and had allowed the whole thing to loom too large in her own life. So she told herself, closing the magazine and putting it on top of the neat pile she had made.

There was just one more on the floor underneath it. This was one of the few French magazines. It had a large coffee stain in the middle of the page, where someone had used it as a coaster under a mug, she thought. Presumably it was unimportant, the page that had been chosen was a gossipy article on celebrities. Katya was smoothing out and closing the magazine when she froze.

She must be jinxed. These magazines must be jinxed. This one too was about Matt, but about him in a very different vein from the adulation of the American review of his music.

Katya ran her eye over it quickly and flinched. Then, forcing herself to be calm, she went back to the beginning and read it slowly.

Matt Saracen, it said with jokey familiarity, was seen in the photograph on page twenty-eight escorting international film star Steffy Solomon in New York at the première of Miss Solomon's latest film for which he had written the score. The music was unlike his earlier work, and there had been particular congratulations on the melting love theme he had written—perhaps, the journalist asked coyly, on the inspiration of lovely Miss Solomon herself?

Miss Solomon, readers were reminded, had been unattached since her divorce from a German banker was made final last year. As for Matt, he had never tied himself down to a permanent relationship before. He liked the bachelor lifestyle, he always said, and his exuberant high spirits had given the authorities in several countries problems in the past. When asked by your reporter, Matt claimed that he and the gorgeous Steffy were very good friends who both liked to party a lot and had some friends in common. Rumours earlier this year of a romance with a mysterious titled lady were dismissed by Matt as 'ridiculous'. He had been working too hard for romance, and now he was playing too hard. Dancing at *Le Giroscope* till five in the morning and leaving after the consumption of heroic numbers of bottles of old Cognac, Matt certainly did not seem to be able to fit in time for love, concluded the article.

Katya let the paper fall in nerveless hands. She felt slightly sick. The door opened and she found herself looking straight into Stacy Alexander's grey eyes. He was no longer smiling.

Conscious of a quivering lip, Katya stared at him, unable to disguise her misery. Stacy Alexander seemed oddly unsurprised by it. He came across to her and twitched the magazine out of her limp fingers, glancing at it critically.

'Trash,' he said dismissively, casting it away from him, his eyes fixed on her.

'I-is it? I'm afraid I don't read it normally . . .' Her voice caught on the suspicion of a sob.

'No, I imagine you don't, or you'd have seen that,' he gestured disparagingly, 'nonsense before.'

She was blank, the violet eyes dark with hurt. 'Why should I have seen it?'

He looked at her levelly. 'Well, you rate a mention in it.' He picked it up and read, '"romance with a mysterious titled lady"' and let it fall again. 'That was you, wasn't it? You're titled, Matt was mysterious and it sounds like one hell of a romance. Want to tell me about it?'

CHAPTER NINE

KATYA said, 'I don't understand.'

She had been saying it, or something very like it, almost hourly. Stacy looked at her in amusement bordering on exasperation. They were sitting at the edge of the open-air ice-rink watching Tom speeding across the ice with all the exuberant confidence of his ten years.

'It's really very simple. Matt is driving himself into the ground. You could do something about it.'

She shook her head helplessly. 'B-but why?'

'You mean why is he driving himself into the ground, or why can you help?'

'Both, I suppose.'

'As to the first, who can say? I can see what he's doing with his all-night parties and his drinking and his eighteen-hour stints at the piano,' he shrugged, 'but I can't tell you *why*. I'm only the boy's f——' he hesitated but finished, 'friend.'

'Is he unhappy?' Katya asked wistfully, not noticing.

'I'd say he was unhappier than I've ever known him,' was the quiet answer.

'Oh!' She looked away across the ice, narrowing her eyes against the glare.

'He's been unreachable. Even since he got back after the summer, nobody can get near him. He drinks too much, works too hard and prickles like a porcupine if anyone tries to talk to him about it.'

Katya knew something about that feverish plunging into work. It helped to swamp the pain by making you too busy to think about it. But surely Matt wouldn't have needed that sort of comfort? She hadn't been the first lady in his life. He must be used to partings. And he had never made any pretence that he wanted anything other than a brief summer affair, so he could not have committed himself and been hurt when the relationship broke down. All that had happened, from his point of view, was that it had ended slightly earlier than he had bargained for.

She said, 'I don't think it can be anything to do with me, you know. Perhaps his work is not going very well.'

There was a little silence, interrupted only by the laughter of the skaters, the hum of conversation from those watching them, an occasional engine starting up in the car park, away to the west of them.

At last he said slowly, 'Yes, that's what I thought at first.'

'Well, then——'

He put up a hand to halt her. 'No, hear me out. I said at first.' He paused, frowning. 'I can tell you when I realised it was more than just a phase of hyperactivity. It was when he turned down Paris.'

Katya stared. Stacy Alexander looked at her gravely.

'He's not just writing well, he's playing superbly. He was due to make some recordings in Philadelphia in September—they got through the sessions in record time, if you'll forgive the pun. So he had some free time. And he told his agent he didn't want a holiday. He'd fulfilled all his commitments and he wanted more. Well,' he shrugged, 'normally tours are booked up months, even years in advance. There wasn't much hope of finding him engagements in the short term, and there he was striding about like a tiger looking for prey. He went and played with a student orchestra, I recall. And then he had this offer: we all breathed a sigh of relief. It was short notice because he would be filling in for another pianist who had been taken ill. The concerts were in Paris.' He stopped.

'And?' Katya prompted.

'And he turned them down. The one thing he wanted was to play and he wouldn't do it in Paris. He said he was never going back there.' Stacy sighed. 'And then he disappeared for thirty-six hours and ended up on the doorstep blind drunk.'

She was horrified. Matt had always seemed so completely in control, particularly of his music. Her heart was moved almost unbearably at the thought of him drunk and helpless, even at the same time as it appalled her.

She shuddered. 'I never saw him drunk, though they told me it happened often.'

'They?' Stacy Alexander took it up swiftly. 'They talked about him to you? Who were *they*?'

'Friends,' Katya said uncommunicatively. 'His as well as mine,' she added, thinking of the Embassy attaché who had looked at her with such pity; such well-deserved pity, as she now realised.

'And you believed them?' He sounded faintly scornful.

Katya stood up, thrusting her hands into the pockets of her coat. She didn't want to discuss Matt any further. The wound was beginning to thaw; the careful restraint she had imposed on herself was beginning to crack. In not too many minutes she would be hurting again, distraught and bereft, begging for news of him, a chance to see him, anything that would feed her unappeasable hunger to be close to him again.

She said coolly, 'Not at first, no, though I probably should have done.'

He stood up too. 'Look, Miss André, I don't want to interfere and I know it's none of my business . . .'

'No,' she agreed and was rewarded with a fierce look.

'I care about Matt. I can't stand by and watch him——'

'Yes? Watch him do what? Go back to his old habits?' she said in a light, chilly voice to disguise the hurt that was roused and raging inside her.

'Burn himself out,' Stacy Alexander said heavily. 'That's what he's doing. Not enough sleep; he's virtually stopped eating; he either locks himself away and works or he's on a wild round of parties. He'll kill himself.'

She flinched, but said scornfully. 'People don't die from an overdose of parties. Presumably he's enjoying himself.'

Stacy Alexander looked down at her, his expression no longer remotely friendly. 'And you don't give a damn,' he said on a long breath.

Katya shrugged. 'Matt Saracen is hardly my responsibility.'

He said almost as if it were a plea, 'Go and see him. If you really don't care it can't matter to you, and it's—at least I think it may be—important to him.'

'You must be mad.' Katya was filled with panic at the very thought.

'Please,' he said.

She was badly shaken. That familiar internal trembling had started at the imagined prospect of seeing Matt again.

'I'm not rich—I can't go dashing off to the States,' she said desperately.

'You don't need to. He's in Europe. He's playing in London.' And as she stared at him in dismay he said eagerly, 'I'll take you to him. He has a concert there the day after tomorrow. I've promised Tom he shall go to London, anyway. We could fly over for the day.' He hesitated, looking embarrassed. 'I'd pay, naturally.'

'No.' It was little more than a whisper. Katya's eyes were enormous in her pinched face and she looked as if she had been confronted with horrors she had never imagined, or so it seemed to the man watching her. The cold had whipped some colouring into the pale cheeks and she looked almost feverish. 'No,' she said

again on a thin high note that sounded like the edge of
hysteria.

And before he could offer further persuasion, she
had turned on her heel and was running, her booted
heels making the impacted snow chip and fly, as if all
the demons of hell were after her.

She walked back to the hotel. The streets were busy
but the covering of snow seemed to muffle sound so
that she felt as if she were walking alone through some
sort of filmed fantasy. All she could hear was her own
harsh breathing and the crunch of her heels on the
snow.

She was miserably bewildered. Was it true that
Matt was behaving out of character? From Stacy
Alexander's account it sounded as if Matt was
suffering almost as much as she was. Yet she found it
impossible to believe.

Unless he had a conscience about what he had done
to her, Katya reminded herself. He had left in a
temper, banging the door behind him after his rapid,
cruel words, but she didn't let that blind her to the
fact that he was not a cruel man. Nor one without
scruples.

Was it that that was now troubling him? Did he fear
that he had damaged her emotionally? Did she owe it
to him to relieve him of that unnecessary anxiety?
And, even if she did, could she bear to see him again?

Head down against the icy breeze, Katya made her
resolute way back to the hotel, no more decided
when she reached it than when she had left Stacy
Alexander.

She moved restlessly round the hotel for the rest of
the day. She ordered coffee she did not want, and
failed to drink it. She set out for a walk and turned
back almost at once. She went down to the lake and
retreated to the pine log fire in the hotel's cheerful
sitting-room. If during this time Stacy Alexander had
telephoned, she would have packed her suitcase and

taken the first flight back to Paris. Because he left her
severely alone, she had time to calm down, to reason
with herself and eventually to decide that one brief
meeting with Matt under the neutral eyes of a third
party could be exactly what they both needed to
restore their sense of balance.

Katya therefore rang him. He picked up the phone
at once, as if he were sitting by it waiting for her call.

'I'll pick you up at three tomorrow,' he said,
expressing neither surprise nor satisfaction when she
told him she'd decided to accept his invitation to
travel to London. 'It'll be too late to come back after
the concert, so we will stay overnight in London.
Leave it all to me.'

She did. But that did not prevent her from acute
anxiety. She checked her slim overnight bag, her
passport and her travellers' cheques fifty times,
though she was a seasoned traveller and seldom gave
such things a thought. And she barely slept.

She was waiting on the shallow steps of the hotel the
next afternoon when Stacy's car drew up. It was a
large saloon with a uniformed chauffeur driving.
Remembering the last time she had sat behind a
chauffeur, Katya suppressed a shiver of apprehension.
It was, she told herself, the height of superstition to
read such things as omens.

The car was the last word in luxury and so was the
small plane in which she and Tom and Stacy were the
only occupants. She said so, observing that though she
was surprised, the boy took it all as perfectly normal.
He even looked slightly disparaging.

'Back home we have our own,' he said matter-of-
factly. 'Dad flies it. He lets me watch. These guys make
you sit down and keep out of the way,' he said in
disgust, having not been welcomed by the uniformed
pilots.

'Do you like flying?' Katya asked, trying to ignore

clammy palms and pounding heart and a growing conviction that she would faint if she so much as set eyes on Matt.

Tom shrugged. 'It's OK. It used to be fun when Matt took me up and looped the loop and things. He's no fun these days, though.'

'I told you, Matt's busy,' Stacy Alexander interrupted, frowning the boy into silence.

Katya said, 'I didn't know,' as always she hesitated over the name, swallowing something painful and jagged in her throat before continuing as steadily as she could manage, 'M-Matt was a pilot.'

'He qualified years ago,' Stacy said, smiling reminiscently. 'He said air fares were costing him a fortune and other people's flying played hell with his nerves. And then he went and hired himself a stunt flyer as an instructor.'

'It doesn't sound very practical,' Katya said faintly.

Stacy laughed. 'Oh, it was practical, okay. It was also a lot of fun. Matt doesn't do things the easy way.'

'Ah,' she said and relapsed into silence.

Throughout the rest of the journey she did try from time to time to make conversation, but as it always, by chance or by Stacy Alexander's deliberate design, came back to Matt, she was always driven back into silence.

They landed at a small airport she did not know, though they told her it was to the west of London. Passport control was perfunctory, though their luggage was searched more thoroughly than she was used to at the major international airports. She saw and was slightly disturbed that Stacy and Tom had brought even less than she had in the way of clothes and night attire. She began to wonder uneasily where they would be staying after the concert.

The question was answered as soon as they reached the metropolis. Another chauffeur-driven car whisked them along the motorway and into the West End. It stopped outside a tall-pillared terrace house in a quiet, leafy street in Holland Park.

'Belongs to a friend of mine,' Stacy said airily. 'I have the run of the basement flat which is kept for guests,' and he produced a key.

The chauffeur unloaded their cases, touched his cap and was told to return at seven-fifteen. As the car departed, Katya had a sudden panicky feeling of having been lured into a trap. She was not at all sure where she was, though it was probably no more than half an hour's walk away from her grandparents' flat. She was not entirely sure that she trusted Stacy, either.

Her suspicions increased when they were inside the flat. It was spotlessly clean with a graceful bowl of flowers in every room; it had clearly been prepared for an honoured guest with some care. The implication, therefore, that Stacy had made the decision to stay here overnight on a spur-of-the-moment impulse, was misleading. Or *had* he implied it? Had she simply jumped to that conclusion?

Katya went to the room that had been assigned to her. It was charming, with a slender vase of creamy freesias on the dressing table, their perfume filling the air. They were beautiful, but her uneasiness re-doubled.

The car came exactly on time. Katya was by then dressed and perfumed and made up to a high degree of sophistication. She was also shaking badly.

Her dress was the one smart one she had taken to Geneva for professorial cocktail parties. It was very simple with a deceptively cut skirt that hung straight and smooth until she turned, when it swirled out like a dance dress. The material was very soft, printed in a gentle blurring of colours from smoke to midnight blue. It made her eyes look huge and violet.

Katya had spent a long time over her make-up. It was understated but it was, as Babette had taught her, perfect. The face that looked back at her from the mirror could have been a model's dressed for a photograph, or an actress's ready for a great performance. Katya smiled wryly, leaning forward to taper an eyebrow. A performance was probably the right word! She would have to act to save her life tonight, and if this mask of a face helped, thank God for it.

It was not an impenetrable mask. There was little to be done to disguise the tension of the cheekbones, though she could and did hide their pallor with matt make-up and delicate blusher. She had outlined her mouth carefully so that it did not look so pinched. The lip-liner emphasised the full lower lip with its hint of passion, thought Katya, faintly surprised at the effect. It made her look both more sensual and more inviting than she was used to. She looked at it doubtfully for a moment, then shrugged. At least it was better than the cold, frightened look her mouth had had before. And her eyes, looking wider than ever under the gold and grey shadow and slightly darkened sooty lashes, were frankly apprehensive.

She shrugged again. She had done her best. If she still looked young and wary there was nothing more to be done about it, unless she could change her character. She went into the hall where the door was open. Stacy waited in his evening clothes and a chauffeur stood on the stone steps with an umbrella.

Stacy's look at her was unrevealing, but, oddly, she thought she heard him say under his breath, 'No wonder', as he took her stole from her and settled it round her shoulders.

The hall was crowded. Katya, a frequent attender at classical concerts, was slightly surprised not just by the number of the audience but by their elegance. There were model dresses and glittering jewels in abundance and more than half the men were in dinner-jackets.

'It's like a charity première,' she said.

Stacy said non-committally, 'The publicity's been good, or so I'm told.'

They had good seats, near the middle of the third row. One or two people looked at Stacy curiously; presumably, thought Katya, they recognised him from the films he had told her about. He was greeted a couple of times, to which he responded graciously but without enthusiasm. He could not have made it plainer that this was a private occasion on which he did not wish to be approached. Tom, wriggling, was almost beside himself with excitement. It occurred to Katya to her surprise, that young Tom hero-worshipped Matt. He could hardly wait for the concert to begin.

The first piece was a short orchestral interlude. Tom stopped wriggling but his applause was polite rather than enthusiastic, and he craned in his seat to peer at the entrance from which, eventually, came Matt.

Katya did not realise she had been holding her breath until she expelled it in a long sigh as he walked to the piano. Her eyes followed him hungrily. He hardly looked at the audience, except for the one obligatory bow to acknowledge the clapping. It was an unsmiling bow.

His expression was so remote that for a moment Katya was almost frightened. She had only seen him look like that once—the day he had left. His facial bones stood out as if they had been etched out of wood with acid. His eyes were hooded. His mouth, which she had so loved, which she remembered in laughter, which she had so often kissed, was a rigid, compressed line. He looked pale and preoccupied.

And when he began to play he was like a man possessed. He hunched over the piano as if it both fascinated and tortured him. He was, obviously, completely oblivious of the audience.

She had never heard him play like it. Suddenly she

recalled the rave review he had received in the American magazine and began to realise what had caused it. This was not a simple improvement, a slight advance on what had already been a flawless technique. This was a sea-change. From somewhere Matthew Saracen had found a depth of emotional intensity which was electrifying. Looking round at the end of the first movement, Katya saw on many faces reflections of what she was feeling herself. They looked stunned; at once humbled and exalted.

'That sort of playing put him up with the masters,' she heard someone say in the interval.

'Ahead of most of them,' said someone else. 'I haven't heard music like that for twenty-five years.'

Katya turned her head slowly to discover who was speaking, but they had moved away. Instead she met Stacy's eyes and realised that he, too, had heard.

She said, 'If that's what happens when he works hard, then it must be worth it. Even if you think he's driving himself.'

'Ah, but he was playing like that before he went into overdrive,' said Stacy. As she stared at him, he went on, 'He didn't change gradually, you know. He went away with one style and he came back different. Playing like that. None of us quite believed it at first. Then we decided something must have happened to him.'

Katya swallowed. 'What happened?'

His voice slowed to a drawl. 'Now I was hoping you would be able to tell me that.'

Her mind whirled. Was he saying that something had happened to Matt in Paris, something to do with her? And if so, what? Guilt? She could imagine that he might have felt guilty, knowing her innocence and unsophistication, quite apart from the unsavoury secret he had kept from her. Or was it something darker than that, something to do with the fury he had shown on that last occasion? Perhaps it was even frustration. He had certainly wanted her, Katya knew that, and he had wanted her willing surrender, which he believed he had never achieved.

She looked down at her hands. Stacy made a swift movement, stilled as the bell went to recall them to the concert hall. She gave a soft sigh, aware of relief.

Stacy touched her arm briefly. 'You'll meet him after the performance,' he said.

And she did. Though it was hardly a meeting, with him surrounded by breathlessly complimentary fans and Katya herself still in a daze of awed delight from his music.

Matt nodded at her over the head of a woman he was talking to: he seemed calm, neither pleased nor displeased to see her. Nor was there any evidence of surprise. Later he stopped beside her.

'In London for Christmas?'

She swallowed. 'No, not exactly.'

'Oh.' His grey eyes held a silvery gleam as they swept the room indifferently. 'Just picking up on culture while you pass through, then?'

Katya knew that she ought to be brave enough to tell him the truth. She should say honestly and without pretence that she had come to London for just this concert, just to see him. She even tried to say it, but she could not. The room was too full, too noisy. Matt was too uninterested and she herself too shaken by what she had heard.

So she gave him a lop-sided smile and agreed she was just picking up on culture.

His eyes stopped wandering round the room then and focused on her, a flame burning in their depths. She took a step backwards, under that concentrated inspection. It might of course be that he was still high on his music and the excitement of performance; that was the most likely cause for that look of glittering intensity. But Katya had a sudden flicker of alarm, as if it was directed at her personally and without any great charity.

'And?' he prompted.

'It was—excellent,' she said lamely, unable to tell him either how the music had moved her.

There was a flash of pure anger, unmistakably, at that. But he said levelly, 'Thank you.'

With horrid brightness, Katya rushed into speech. 'They tell me you're really on top form these days. I heard people raving about you in the interval.'

Matt's expression was ironical. 'True. Are you having second thoughts, darling?'

She jumped, flushing. 'I don't know what you mean.'

'No?' He looked round again at the room, full of diamonds and Paris originals. 'Did you come to any of my concerts before they got on the social calendar?'

'You haven't played in Paris,' she protested, defending herself.

'We are not,' said Matt, reaching for another drink and pouring it into the quarter-full glass he already held, 'in Paris now.' He swallowed the drink in one go and gave her a mocking look. 'Your family runs true to form, I see. Never let a bandwagon pass!'

Katya was hurt and did not know how to disguise it. 'You don't understand.'

'Don't I?' The grey eyes were brilliant with rage and drink, and a more primitive emotion that Katya recognised. He pinched her chin, insulting her. 'I think I understand very well. I'll even co-operate. Stick around, darling. I'll see you when the hyenas have gone.'

He reached for another drink from a side table. He must have found it by touch alone, Katya thought, for he never took his eyes from her face. She felt scorched by the naked desire she read in them. It frightened her; but nevertheless, deep in the centre of her body she felt something wake and flex and yearn towards him. And that frightened her more than anything else.

She put her own glass down without a word, and turned and left him. She knew, without looking, that he never took his eyes off her and that he was incandescent with fury at her rejection. Stacy, taking in both her rigid face and Matt's expression, sighed deeply and gave her a front door key. She didn't have to say a word.

She took a taxi back to the flat, let herself in and went at once to bed. She was shaking so badly by the time she got there that it took her ten minutes to unhook her clothes. She crawled under the covers, hunched herself into a tight ball like a squirrel for its hibernation, and willed herself to sleep.

Katya came awake, wide awake, suddenly. She did not know why, there was no obvious sound to account for it, though she lay in bed with straining ears. At first she thought it must be Stacy and Tom—perhaps they had no other key and she had locked them out. She listened. But no, all was quiet. The small bedside alarm-clock with which the room was furnished said three-fifteen on its illuminated dial.

Then, very softly, almost surreptitiously, it came again; the noise of an unsteady hand fumbling at a door. Katya sat up in bed and put her light on. It did not sound very alarming now that she was awake. It sounded rather pathetic. She wondered whether Stacy or the boy was ill, and the thought disturbed her. At last, reaching a decision, she got up and slipped her arms into the man-sized velour robe she had found on the back of the door.

Then she padded out into the hallway. It was quite dark. The fumbling was clearer out here. It came from a panelled door at the end of the passage. She had noticed it earlier in the evening but did not know where it led. It was certainly not either Stacy's or Tom's room, nor the bathroom she had used earlier. Very cautiously, she eased it open.

On the other side, swaying in a dim light from a distant lamp, stood Matthew Saracen. He was wearing a raincoat with snow on its shoulders, a raffish white silk scarf flung anyhow round his neck, and the evening clothes in which he had given his performance, now much crumpled. His eyes burned like coals. When she opened the door he looked almost startled. Then, bracing himself against the door frame with each hand, he leaned forward confidentially and murmured her name.

Katya was by now wide awake and, for all her lack of sophistication, she had never been a fool. 'Have you been drinking?' she asked in resignation, taking in his appearance.

'Lots,' he agreed nodding. 'Lots and lots and lots.' He lurched forward, throwing his arms about her, so that she staggered. 'Tired. Want to sleep.'

Katya put her arms out instinctively to support him. She could well believe he was tired. His face looked drawn and, in spite of the insouciance engendered by alcohol, she could sense a terrible tension in the taut body under her hands. She said gently, 'You must lie down, Matt. Get some rest.'

He kissed her long and lovingly. 'You're a wonderful girl, do you know that? A wonderful, understanding girl. Rest. Yes.'

'Thank you,' said Katya. 'Repeat that when you're sober and I'll count myself flattered.' The casual kiss had stirred memories of passion, not for the first time that night, and she reached hard for common sense. Matt did not know where he was nor, probably, who he was with. She mustn't delude herself that all was well between them because, just for the moment, he was here and he was holding her and he did not seem hostile.

'Sleep,' he said longingly, his head drooping on to her shoulder.

'Yes,' she agreed, her mind working.

It was obviously hopeless to try to get him out of the flat and back to wherever it was he lived. He was almost asleep on his feet as it was, quite apart from the fuddle of drink. She looked round distractedly. There was any number of doors off this dark corridor but she could not guess which, if any, led to spare rooms. She made a decision.

'Come along,' she said, guiding him into the room she had occupied.

He blinked in the light, looking round him like an awakening child. Katya unwound his scarf and drew the overcoat from his unresisting shoulders.

'Your room,' said Matt, with some apparent return of clarity.

'Yes, but it doesn't matter. I know there's a sofa in the sitting-room. And I can spend the rest of the night there.' She gave him a grin, suddenly oddly happy to be with him in this slightly ridiculous predicament, helping him and loving him. She kissed his cheek, laughing softly. 'Your need is greater than mine just at this moment, I think.'

He shook his head, not as if he was denying what she said but as if he was trying to clear it by shaking away the fog of alcohol and weariness. He sank down on to the end of the bed, clasping his head between his hands.

'Water,' he said.

Katya looked at him doubtfully, but went to get what he asked. At least she knew where the bathroom was and could find a tooth-mug there. She came back with it. Matt took the mug silently and drained it. Then he straightened, pushing a hand through his wildly tousled red hair.

'More?' asked Katya.

'Yes, but—I'll get it,' he was enunciating carefully.

He stood up and staggered. She instinctively reached out a hand to him. He caught it and held it against his breast for a moment. Then, looking down at her with that unreadable smile, he let her go.

'It's all right. I need to—sober up a little.' His voice slurred and he stopped dead. *'Damn!'*

Katya looked at him anxiously. 'Are you all right? Had I better come with you?'

Matt touched her face briefly, as if he could not bear not to.

'Better not. I'm going to splash a bit.' He ran a thumb, not entirely steadily, along her bottom lip. 'Get back into bed, you'll be cold. I'll come back when I can see straight.'

She was still anxious, but Matt was right when he said she would get cold. She was shivering. So she did as he said and hopped back into bed, pulling the duvet up to her chin.

Matt surveyed her from the doorway, a smile in his eyes. 'And don't go to sleep,' he warned softly.

Katya had seldom been so far from sleep in her life. She pushed the pillows up behind her and sat up, twining her fingers together. She was in a fever of anticipation for him to return, at the same time as she was terrified. He had been so natural, so affectionate in those few exchanges. What if, when he rid himself of the effect of alcohol, he rid himself of those gentle feelings as well? What if he came back angry and resentful as he had been at that party? What if—she shut her eyes tight at the agony of the thought—he did not come back at all?

A voice from the doorway, still soft but now steadier and full of amusement, made her eyes fly open. 'I *told* you not to go to sleep,' said Matt, advancing.

She watched him, violet eyes huge. He must have plunged his head under water because his hair was dark with it, and the shoulders of his shirt were sopping. His tie had gone, his shirt was open to the waist and the cuffs were flying. Katya was assailed by a heady combination of feelings, all of them urging her to reach out and touch him. She swallowed, terrified of her reaction.

Matt bent to her, taking her face between his hands. 'Katya, my lovely one, don't look so frightened,' he scolded gently. 'I'm quite sober now, I won't hurt you.'

Her throat moved again. 'I believe you,' she whispered, meeting his eyes steadily, though she could not disguise her shyness.

His mouth twisted. 'Do you? Can you prove it?'

There was a sudden, heart-stopping silence. Katya found that she was on the edge of a precipice without any clear idea of how she had got there. Matt's expression was no longer unreadable. He looked tortured. She could read terrible uncertainty in his eyes, dark now almost to jet, and though the hands cradling her face were gentle, they shook with their own urgency. It was, she realised, within her power to remove the torture, respond to the urgency, reassure the uncertainty.

She unfolded her twisting hands and, reaching up to him, slipped them under his shirt, so that they moved on his shoulders, drawing the garment away from him.

'Come to bed, Matt,' she said quietly.

CHAPTER TEN

AFTERWARDS she marvelled at the naturalness of it. It seemed as if it was what she had been waiting for ever since they had met; all her life, even. It seemed inevitable. There was none of that half-fearful excitement which had tormented her in Paris. There was just love.

Matt looked at her in lingering disbelief. 'Are you sure, Katya?'

'Yes,' she said calmly. Because she was.

He began to kiss her then, not gently at all, with a hunger that neither of them made any attempt to deny. He murmured her name over and over again, straining her against him so fiercely that a metal fastening on the robe she wore dug into her. She made a small, breathless protest and sat once he loosed her, looking at her with anxiety.

'What is it? What did I do?'

Katya gave a little laugh. 'Not you, my darling, my borrowed dressing-gown,' she said, showing him the mark it had made. He leaned forward and brushed his lips against it very delicately.

'I'm sorry. I'm a clumsy brute.'

'Don't be ridiculous,' she said, and broke off with a gasp as she found that he was no longer kissing the little indentation, that his lips were travelling very softly along the curve of her breast, while he drew away the restricting garments she was wearing to free a path for his kisses. Katya shuddered under his touch, speechless.

'And you're wearing too many clothes,' he told her, laughing against her skin. 'This thing is probably full of hooks and eyes. Or safety pins. Even old razor blades. It is,' he coaxed, mock-solemn, 'in your own *interests* to take it off.'

'Quite,' said Katya appreciatively, doing so.

She paused and then, shyly, shrugged out of her nightdress as well. Matt looked up then and for a long moment gazed into her eyes.

'Katya——'

She leaned forward, kissing him hard, all the suppressed feeling of months welling up and demanding expression.

'I love you,' she said harshly.

The laughter went then. His eyes darkened and he turned, taking away the covering of bedclothes and nightdress and replacing them with his warm, worshipping mouth. Katya shut her eyes tight at the new and glorious sensations he was arousing. In intensity they were almost like pain, but she did not hurt, she was shaking with pleasure.

And she pleased him too. She could tell from his uneven breathing, the occasional ragged gasp when a spontaneous touch of hers moved him. She might be inexperienced, but she loved him and she was overwhelmed by the exquisite concern that he was lavishing on her awakening body. She clung to him, moving against him, responding without reserve.

Once he raised his head, shaking the hair out of his eyes, and looked down at her. 'I never thought . . .' he said, and then, in a rush, half groaning, 'Oh God, Katya, you've torn the heart out of me.'

Suddenly his hands were mastering her body, so that she was no longer her own creature but his, and instead of fearing or resenting the sensation, she sobbed with the unexpected delight of it. She rose to meet him fiercely, murmuring his name over and over again, half plea, half command. Then at last he took her into the final phase of sensation that she had never even imagined before. It was like breaking through clouds into sunshine. She soared in golden pleasure, unaware of anything but the absolute rightness of their bodies together and the profound companionship of the moment. Matt was her friend, her lover, her only security in a dangerous world, her fellow and the one man who could match her. Katya felt utterly fulfilled. Holding him against her with passion, she did not even know that there were tears on her face.

She woke slowly to a feeling of delicious comfort. She was warm and languorous. She moved slightly and found that she was lying with her head on Matt's shoulder; as she moved his arm, which was round her, the hand lying softly on her hip tightened into an iron bar. Katya turned her head and looked up into his eyes, smiling. Matt's grey eyes glinted down at her.

'Awake at last?' he teased. 'I thought you would sleep through the day.'

Katya grinned and stretched, loving the feeling of her body moving under his fingertips.

'Can't afford to,' she said. 'We've got to get up and get you back to your own abode, wherever that may be.'

He stroked her side absently. 'No need to worry about that yet.'

Katya hauled herself up on her elbow and peered at the clock. 'Oh yes, there is. Look at the time. My host will be waking me up for breakfast at any moment.'

Matt smoothed back the hair from her face in a proprietorial gesture. 'There is no way my father would put his nose round that door until we get up,' he said in amusement.

Katya went very still. 'Y-your father?'

'The man you know as Stacy Anderson,' he told her. 'It's a sort of pen-name of his. He writes children's stories under it, anyway. But he is really Saracen Senior—Brett Saracen, star of stage, screen and Geneva Hotels.'

Katya said carefully. 'Are you telling me that he lied to me?'

Matt shrugged. 'A little harmless deception, perhaps.'

She removed herself from his encircling arm. 'Like your own?' she asked politely.

The grey eyes grew watchful. 'Mine?'

'The little matter of omitting to mention you had fathered my cousin's child,' said Katya in a light, cold voice. It was suddenly all flooding back to her with appalling clarity. He might seem to love her, he might carry her to the stars with him, but beneath it all was the calculating sensualist who pursued what he wanted without scruple. 'Or that you live here, which I assume you must do, if Stacy is your father?'

She got out of bed and scrabbled for her clothes. Her nightdress had disappeared, but the borrowed robe was found easily enough where Matt had dropped it beside the bed last night. She struggled into it and belted it tightly while Matt watched her without speaking. She swung back to him, her mouth rigidly controlled to prevent it trembling.

'Well?' she challenged.

'Yes, I live here,' Matt said slowly, 'though I don't see why it's important. Or to be more precise, I live in the house. Dad uses the flat when he's in town, so he keeps a key.' He shrugged. 'So do other people.'

Including Steffy Solomon? she wondered in anguish, turning away so he should not see her expression.

His voice roughened. 'It's no sinister plot, you know. This is just an ordinary guest flat. You haven't been kidnapped. You can walk out of it whenever you like.'

'Good,' she said viciously, moving to the door. 'I'll be going as soon as I've dressed.'

'Why?'

'Why?' She swung round on him, hair flying, eyes furious. 'You dare to ask me why? When you sent your father to spy on me, had me brought here, manipulated me . . .'

'Made love to you,' he reminded her softly, interrupting.

She stopped dead, losing all colour.

'How can you remind me of that?' she said in a stifled voice. 'Aren't you *ashamed*?'

He stretched lazily, putting his arms up behind his head, watching her from narrowed eyes. 'No, I think I'm rather proud of myself,' he said reflectively.

Katya winced. She felt as if he had picked up a javelin and casually lobbed it at her, transfixing her through the heart. She picked up her clothes from the basket chair where she had left them the night before.

'Then allow me to congratulate you,' she said coolly, not looking at him.

Matt gave a soft laugh which made her blush burningly. He didn't care. He didn't care at all. That laugh, that idly lounging body, as graceful as a satisfied cat, said it all. He had been annoyed with her in Paris because she had asked him to leave, but now he had his revenge and was plainly delighted with it. He was looking at her as if he was savouring the memory of every abandoned moment she had spent in his arms last night; every unguarded word. She had never hurt so badly in her life.

Katya said, 'I'm going to wash.'

Matt gave a grin. 'I shall give my father a wad of sterling pound notes and tell him to take Tom to the zoo. Then you and I will have a long, leisurely breakfast, during which I make no promises not to make love to you again, and we'll talk.'

'Yes,' Katya said woodenly, hardly hearing him.

She went rapidly from the room, showered and dressed and made her way silently into the sitting-room. There were signs that Stacy and Tom had been there earlier, although the flat now sounded as empty as a locked church. Presumably they had stolen out quietly in order not to waken her. She wondered whether Stacy had known or guessed that she was in bed with his son, and felt choked in a wave of humiliation at the thought. Presumably they had schemed together to that end; Stacy must have concluded that their machinations had been successful, she thought, biting her lip.

She could not bear to see either of them again. She could not. She checked her handbag. She had her passport but very little money, none of it English. She had her credit cards, though, if anywhere was open in this holiday period to accept them. Somehow, anyhow, she would get herself away from here, back to Geneva for the rest of her holiday; failing that she would go back to Paris and go straight to work. She could not face Matt and that mocking triumph of his which had turned last night into a travesty of the love that she had brought to it.

She picked up her bag and let herself quietly out of the flat. There was no sound behind her.

In the end Katya went to her cousin Paul's. She could have gone to her grandparents, she knew, but she could not face their inquisition. They would be convinced that this proved their point that grand-daughters ought to stay at home until they married suitable young men. Paul, at least, would not crow.

Paul was, in fact, very much more sympathetic than that. One look at Katya's pinched face and shocked eyes and he handed her over to his wife to be put to bed with hot milk, waving away her protestations that she didn't want to be a nuisance. They were delighted to see her. The children would be overjoyed to thank her for their Christmas presents in person when she eventually got up, but for now she was to sleep and not to worry about anything. The grandparents, said Paul meaningly, were going to dinner with friends that evening, so the family was not expected at the flat in

Campden Hill Road.

'Thank you, Paul,' Katya said in a small voice, and burst into tears.

She was hurried off into the room of the youngest child where she slept, eventually, with her arms wrapped round herself and her head, incongruously, pillowed on the stout stomach of a grubby teddy bear. Awaking for the second time that day in a strange bed, Katya was instantly aware of a sense of devastating loss. She reached for Matt instinctively, and came fully awake as the bear fell squashily to the floor.

She sat up, passing a hand over her bleary eyes. She felt drained and faintly sick, though she knew she had to pull herself together for the sake of Paul, Anna and the children. When a light tap came at the door, she braced herself, dredging up a welcoming smile.

But it was not Paul. Nor was it kind, concerned Anna; nor the small owner of the dispossessed bear. Stepping cautiously into the room came a vision in burnt orange pedal-pushers and tiger-striped jerkin, beautiful face exquisitely made up and rather apprehensive.

'*Vonnie!*' gasped Katya, surprise and affection in her first startled greeting.

Princess Irena looked relieved. 'Oh, good, you're awake, darling. Paul said I wasn't to disturb you.'

'You didn't,' Katya assured her. 'I'd already kicked Teddy out of bed and woke myself doing it.'

Vonnie bent and picked up the bear, smiling wryly. She smoothed his fur and restored him to Katya before perching gracefully on the side of the little bed.

'I expect he deserved it,' she said, watching Katya tuck the toy under the borrowed covers. 'He's not much of a substitute.'

Katya tensed. She had a little suspicion that Vonnie's appearance was not wholly by chance and she did not want to discuss Matt with his former lover, fond though she was of her cousin.

'Substitute?' she echoed wearily.

Vonnie's expression was full of irony. 'At your age, darling, even good little girls like you don't want to be sleeping with stuffed animals. Or so I imagine.'

Katya relaxed, even laughed a little. 'Sometimes it's all that good little girls like me are offered,' she pointed out.

Vonnie did not laugh in return. She was frowning, looking more serious than Katya had ever seen her. 'Not you, sweetie. You're a stunner. If you didn't have your nose buried in Bunsen burners all the time, you'd know that.' She fumbled in her shoulder bag and brought out an amber cigarette holder. She did not light a cigarette, though, just played with it, turning it over and over in her gold-tipped fingers. 'That's one of the reasons Grandmama was always so hard on you. Partly because of me, of course.'

Katya said nothing, now positive that this visit had a purpose.

Vonnie put the holder down and wandered to the window. With her back to Katya she said, 'They come from another world, Katya. They mean well. You can't blame them.'

Katya closed her eyes briefly. 'I don't,' she said, and then, reminding herself, turning the knife in her own wound, she added, 'At least they told me the truth.'

Vonnie clearly misunderstood, taking the comment to reflect on herself. Of course, she knew very little of Katya's dealings with Matt, whatever she might have been told by Paul or suspect for herself. She hung her head now, looking miserable.

'I know. You should have been told—I should have told you. Only at the time I was young and silly and in a panic and I just did what the grandparents told me. Blindly.' She gave Katya a very straight look. Her cousin was astonished to see that Vonnie's lovely eyes were swimming in tears. Vonnie, the hard sophisticate, never cried. 'I've regretted—many things, since.'

'I wish I'd known,' Katya said softly. 'It must have been hard for you.'

Vonnie shuddered, twisting one of the heavy gold rings she wore on every finger. Katya wondered whether any or all of her wedding rings were included in the collection.

She said drily, 'I was spoilt and silly and I expect I deserved it, though I would give different advice to a girl in that position, if anyone asked me. But you should have been told. And if Grandmama wouldn't do it, I should have done. I can see that.'

Compassionately Katya said, 'Oh, Vonnie, it was your life. You had a right to do what you wanted.'

'Not when it affected you too. And it did, I knew it did. When I saw them keeping you in at night, not letting you go to a proper school, trying to stop you going to university . . .' She sighed heavily. 'I should have said something then. You were being punished for my foolishness, and it was unfair. And now——'

Katya tensed. Her cousin looked ill at ease.

'Paul says—that is, he told me that he thought—that Grandmama has stopped you seeing Matt Saracen.'

Katya shook her head. 'I'm not a child any more, Vonnie. *I* stopped me seeing Matt Saracen.'

'But because of what Grandmama told you?' pursued Vonnie, undeflected.

'And because of what Matt had not told me.'

Her cousin looked even more unhappy. 'I suppose he felt that it wasn't for him to tell,' she murmured. 'He was probably protecting us—well, me, to be honest. He was always like that: ready to take it all on himself.'

Katya moved sharply. The thought of Matt protecting the good name of the woman he once loved was extraordinarily hurtful, she found. She tried to suppress the unworthy feeling.

Vonnie went on, 'But that's not fair, either. It wasn't Matt's responsibility. I ought to tell you myself.'

Katya stared. 'Not Matt's responsibility?' she echoed. 'When you had his *child*?'

It was Vonnie's turn to look blank. 'What are you talking about?'

Katya said wearily, 'Grandmama told me in the end. And Matt didn't deny it.'

'That Matt was the father of my child?'

Katya nodded. Vonnie came away from the window and put her arms round her cousin.

'You poor little soul! No wonder you thought the end of the world had come. Our respected grandmother is a calculating old crone, and never forget it. There isn't a word of truth in it,' she said firmly.

Katya raised her head. Vonnie answered her unspoken question. 'God knows what Matt thought he was about, not telling you the truth, but I will. When I was silly and starstruck I had an affair with Matt's *father*. When I found I was pregnant Brett wanted to marry me, but the grandparents wouldn't hear of it. I,' she admitted, 'was in hysterics most of the time. And there were medical complications. I more or less went into the clinic and let the grandparents get on with it. That was hard on Brett. He was the one worst hit, I think, in the end. He had this complex about not being a proper father to Matt after the divorce, and he desperately wanted marriage and children. He had some sort of breakdown, I believe. I wasn't told, of course,' she added bitterly. 'I only found out by accident, years later. But that would account for why Matt handled all the practical things—money, you know, and having the boy adopted.'

How can she talk about it so calmly, thought Katya, as if it happened to someone else.

As if she sensed the thought, Vonnie said with a twisted smile, 'I was a different person then. Terribly immature, though I thought I was so dashing, having an affair with an older man. I never realised how important it might be to him. And as for the child—

well I was little more than a child myself. I didn't know what to do with it. Now of course it would be different, but now——' she gave a little, painful shrug'—I've burned my boats. I won't get a second chance. But that has nothing to do with you, Katya. You mustn't let my mistakes spoil your life.'

Katya said, 'What do you mean?' though she knew very well.

'If you love Matt you must go to him,' Vonnie said soberly. 'Never mind the grandparents. Never mind me and my rotten past. Matt is what matters, if you care for him.

'Even if he doesn't care for me?' asked Katya in a sad little voice.

Vonnie looked astonished. 'Doesn't he?'

Katya shook her head decisively. 'He wanted me, all right. He was annoyed when I got away. But when I first saw him last night he said I'd come back because he was famous these days.'

Vonnie's eyes, so like her own, narrowed. 'And later?'

'Later?'

'You said,' pointed out Vonnie with patience, 'when you *first* saw him: so what happened when you next saw him?'

Katya said nothing, but a slow tide of delicate colour washed up under her skin. Her eyes fell.

'I see,' said Vonnie in amusement. 'He doesn't care for you, he thought you were celebrity-chasing, so he took you to bed. My dear child, you're bats.'

But Katya refused to be comforted. 'He didn't say he loved me. He has *never* said he loved me,' she said. 'And he never trusted me enough to tell me the truth about you and the child.' The lovely eyes rose, dark as rainwashed lavender. 'So he can't love me, can he?' she concluded simply.

CHAPTER ELEVEN

KATYA went back to Paris at the end of the first week of January. Paul and Anna had persuaded her to stay with them over the Twelfth Night Festival and even to see her grandparents, though that was not a very jolly evening.

Prince Casimir had arrived full of indignant determination that Katya should now return to London to her rightful place in their home. He was speedily disabused by Katya herself.

'I'm going back to Paris to finish my contract, Grandpapa,' she said quietly, 'and then I shall go on somewhere else, wherever I get a job. My work is important to me.'

He began to bluster. It could not be important. It was not right that a woman should work, still less a princess. She should grow up, recognise her responsibilities, come home and marry someone suitable.

Katya rounded on him. 'You and my grandmother have ensured that I will *never* marry,' she flared at him in an uncharacteristic display of emotion.

Prince Casimir was taken aback. More, he was frightened. Katya might not have been as docile as he would have liked, but she had never had a temper. The only temper in the house had been his own. He said in slightly flustered dignity that he only wanted what was best for her, and discovered that the lovely violet eyes could be unduly penetrating.

'Did you send my grandmother to Paris to talk me out of seeing Matt Saracen?' Katya demanded shrewdly.

His expression of guilt was blatant. Katya nodded her head.

'I thought so. And presumably you also told her to let me think that Vonnie's affair had been with Matt?'

'She saw a lot of him,' said Prince Casimir defiantly.

'In his father's house, she tells me,' Katya returned, unmoved. 'You deceived me, you and Grandmama. Rather cleverly. I may perhaps forgive you in time, I don't know, but I shall certainly never come back and share your home again. And for the time being I think it would be better if we did not meet,' she concluded quietly. She stood up, dismissing him, more regal than he had ever imagined his egalitarian granddaughter could be. 'Goodbye, Grandpapa.'

He went. He could not convince himself that she did not mean it, though he tried. He put his trust, therefore, in his wife's remonstrances. But the Princess fared no better.

'You let me think that Matt had lied to me,' Katya accused. 'When all the time it was you who was lying. How *could* you?'

The Princess quailed, as her husband had done, before this new, impassioned but self-possessed granddaughter.

'My darling, the publicity,' she protested feebly. 'The press can be so unkind. And, though you don't like to be reminded of it, you are a Princess Andreyevna . . .' She was interrupted.

'Get out,' said Katya with a ferocity that was nonetheless intimidating for being softly spoken.

And the Princess, who had never been spoken to in that way in her life before, not by anyone, let alone a respectful and nicely-brought-up granddaughter, retreated in horror.

Later Katya relented enough to write to them. She spent considerable time and thought on the letter, though in the end she was hardly satisfied with it. She was not at all sure that they would realise, even now, the extent of the injury they had done her, though she did her best to point out the damage that their meddling in her life had brought about. Not least to themselves, she said, since she felt her relationship with them had been irreparably damaged. They could, however, be assured that she was not about to go off on a wild round of debauchery to console herself for the loss of what would have been the most important relationship in her life. Nevertheless, in future she would not permit them to comment on or influence her conduct in any way, and if they tried she would cut them out of her life completely and permanently.

She posted it from Paris, after her return. If she had posted it in London, Prince Casimir would have descended, shouting and bullying and, though Katya was no longer distressed by the scenes he caused, she did not want to inflict one on Paul and his kind wife. As she posted it from Paris they were all safe.

She did not hear from Matt. Though she watched the post anxiously and never failed to enquire on returning to her room whether there was a telephone message for her, nothing ever came. She concluded that he had got whatever obscure satisfaction it was that he sought from her, and had no further use for her. She tried to tell herself that she was pleased, that at least she had managed to remove herself from his life without having to be told to go.

The magazines in the common room—for of course she would not buy such nonsense herself—reported him to be happily accompanying Steffy Solomon on her European tour publicising the Columbus film. Katya believed it. In the photographs they looked relaxed and happy together.

It came as something of a shock, therefore, to learn that he was coming to Paris. The advertisements said that it was the first concert of a European tour. Katya remembered that Stacy Alexander had told her that Matt refused categorically to come to Paris, and took this as yet another sign that he had finished with whatever feelings he had had about their time together. She got herself a ticket, but vowed that she would not get in touch with him if he did not seek her out himself. He did not.

The decision, however, was not left entirely in her hands either. She came home early on the night of the concert. Henri had shouted at her that if she could not keep her mind on the job she should go home, after she broke the third glass test tube in a row. When she pushed open the door of her apartment building she discovered that she had a visitor, though it wasn't Matt.

'Hi,' said the Embassy's cultural attaché, strolling forward casually as if they met every day and he had entirely forgotten the home truths he told her on the last occasion. 'Your *concierge* said I could wait for you, Miss André, I hope you don't mind. I missed you at work.'

Katya took off her rain-soaked scarf, shaking the falling cloud of hair. She was puzzled, and she said so.

'Yes, it must seem odd,' he admitted. 'It's Saracen, you see.'

Katya did not move a muscle. She was proud of her raised eyebrows and the steady voice in which she said, 'Matthew Saracen?'

'Yes. He's playing in Paris tonight—I hope——' he added under his breath, 'and I have a bit of a problem with him.'

Katya was taking off her raincoat. 'And that has something to do with me?' she asked, injecting just the right note of scornful incredulity into her tone.

He looked rueful. 'Yes, I know it's a cheek, but I'm at my wits' end, Miss André. He's behaving like a child. I've got him to the concert hall but he's lowering whisky like there's no tomorrow and saying he won't go on.' He paused, looking uncomfortable. 'Or not unless you're there.'

Katya was genuinely startled. She stopped play-acting and gaped at him.

'Look, would you come over there with me, now?' he asked in a rush. 'Somehow I've got to get him on to that stage and I don't reckon much to my chances unless you come along. I've seen him difficult,' he added, 'but I've never seen him like this before. And he always leaves his drinking till after the performance. At least, he always has done before. But this time he's in a sort of crazy mood—I can't do anything with him and neither can his father. We really need you, Miss André, believe me.'

She didn't know that she went quite so far as to do that, but she certainly could not resist such a plea. She turned and went with him immediately, not pausing even to change out of her wet things or collect her own ticket for the concert.

The artists' entrance of the concert hall was a strictly functional single-barred door at the end of an uncarpeted corridor. A man put his head out of a small booth behind the door and, seeing them, nodded them on.

'Still there?' asked Katya's companion, looking anxious.

'Yes,' agreed the man impassively. 'And he's had another three bottles sent up.'

'Oh, God,' groaned the American.

He put a hand under Katya's elbow and rushed her along corridors and up ill-lit staircases until she was breathless. Eventually they came to a grim, grey-painted door, no less depressing than the rest of this side of the building, in sharp contrast to the lavishness of the auditorium, thought Katya, who knew it. Her companion knocked perfunctorily on the door and went in at once, half dragging her with him.

Matt was lying in an attitude of abandon on a green velvet chaise-longue. The dark auburn hair was tousled and his eyes were closed. He was wearing his dress trousers and a frilled white shirt but no attempt had been made to button the shirt and his coat was flung carelessly across another chair. Two whisky bottles, ominously empty, stood on the floor beside one loosely outflung hand. He did not move at their entrance.

The man Katya still thought of as Stacy appeared from a far doorway. He was looking tense, carrying a cloth which he was squeezing carefully between his hands, but when he saw her his expression lightened noticeably.

'Katya, my dear.' He came across to her, then hesitated as if he didn't know whether to embrace her or not. He gave her a cautious smile. 'It is good of you to come.'

She took in Matt's recumbent form with a feeling of helplessness. Obviously they expected that now she was here she would work some magic spell, which would get Matt up on his feet and fit to play for the enormous audience that would soon begin to filter into the concert hall. And she had no idea how to go about it. She looked at him again, biting her lip.

Her companion went across to Matt and shook him by the shoulders hard. 'Wake up man. You've got to get moving.'

Matt stirred, murmuring something unintelligible.

'Wake *up*. I've even got the girl, for God's sake. Now *move*, damn you.'

Matt shifted, hunching a shoulder against his tormentor. Jack stepped back with a look of despairing entreaty at Katya.

'See what I mean? He's been like that ever since I got here.'

Katya went and knelt down by the couch. She lifted Matt's unresisting hand from the floor. It was cool to the touch, he didn't seem to be running any sort of temperature. She dusted her hand gently across his forehead, more because she could not help herself than for any sound reason.

'Matt,' she said firmly, 'will you please stop making an ass of yourself and sit up,' and she slapped him smartly on the cheek.

The effect was gratifying, if unexpected. He sat bolt upright and glared at her. Behind her, Katya heard Stacy gasp. The American attaché began to laugh, though, after a moment.

'Thank you, Princess,' Matt said in an icy tone, not slurring his words in the slightest. 'Perhaps you will ask your retinue to get out and leave us alone.'

'Oh, no,' began Katya alarmed, swinging round on her knees to look imploring at Stacy.

But it was too late. The older man, too, was beginning to contemplate his son with dawning amusement.

'Yes. I'm—er—sure you'll be better on your own,' he agreed, ignoring Katya's pleading expression. 'Come on, Jack. We'll see you later, Matt.'

The door closed behind them as Katya sprang to her feet in agitation. She would have followed had Matt not prevented her by the simple expedient of reaching out and taking hold of her wrist. His fingers were long and delicate, but as they flexed about the bones of her wrist she was made to feel their strength. She stood where she was, feeling resentful and refusing to look at him.

'Sit down,' said Matt pleasantly but with great firmness.

'I won't,' flared Katya. 'Did you bring me here to make a fool of me?'

He tugged at her wrist and she collapsed on to the edge of his chaise-longue. 'I brought you here so we could both stop being fools.'

'I don't know what you mean,' said Katya, trying to retrieve her hand.

'Yes, you do,' he contradicted maddeningly.

She made an infuriated sound. 'Oh, I'm not going to sit here arguing with you . . .'

Matt gave a soft chuckle. 'Good,' he said, and tipped her back so that she was held helpless against the couch, and kissed her thoroughly.

When at last he raised his head he was breathing hard and Katya's eyes were round with amazement. 'You don't taste of whisky at all,' she accused him. 'I don't believe you've had a drink all evening.'

He grinned down at her, caressing her face as if he could never bear to leave it alone.

'Quite right.'

'But—but why?'

He looked shocked. 'I never drink before a concert. It's unprofessional,' he said with infuriating smugness.

'I could,' said Katya wistfully, 'hit you.'

'No, no, you've already hit me once this evening, my darling. Which I may say,' he admitted, 'I hadn't expected.'

'It was entirely your own fault,' Katya said virtuously. 'I thought you were in a drunken stupor.'

He hugged her. 'I acknowledge it.'

'Then you can jolly well acknowledge why you put up this whole charade,' said Katya with heat.

'Ah. That was my final throw. A sort of Saracen's last stand.'

'*What?*'

'You wouldn't speak to me. Didn't answer my letters. It was all I could think of.'

Katya stared. 'What letters?'

Matt said, 'The ones I've been sending daily to Campden Hill Road.'

Katya struggled to sit up, putting her fingers to her temples. She felt as if her head was ringing. 'You've been writing to me at my grandparents' address? But why?'

'I've been writing to you because I was desperate to see you,' Matt said evenly. 'To that address because that's where I assumed you went after you—left me, that day. And when I rang, your grandmother

admitted you were there. And you never went back to
Geneva to collect your bags. You just settled the bill
from London. I checked.'

'I see.' Katya expelled a long breath. 'And
Grandmama told you I was with them?'

'She said you were too upset to see me or anyone
and would not be returning to Paris. As I knew that
you'd finished your thesis——'

'How did you know that?' Katya gasped.

Matt shrugged, his smile twisted. 'I checked,' he
said again. 'I've spied. I've kept asking. You wouldn't
believe how close I kept to you last year. It was only
because there wasn't any sign of another man on the
horizon that I stayed away. If Kolkanin had shown his
face, I would have been back.'

Katya shook her head in bewilderment. 'I would
never have believed it,' she agreed ruefully. 'You
seemed so distant, somehow. So remote and sophisticated——'

She broke off as Matt flung up a hand. 'Don't,' he
said, 'don't say any more. At least, not until I've told
you some of the important things.'

The fun had died out of his face now. He looked
drawn again and tired, as he had done after his recital
in London, and desperately sober. He took her hands
and held them, palm upwards, studying them
absorbedly.

At last he began, 'I really thought you were in
London. God forgive me, even after all this time it
didn't occur to me that your grandmother might be
lying. It seems sacrilege to think of untruth in
connection with such a gracious lady, I suppose. So I
didn't look for you in Paris as I should have done.
Forgive me for that.'

Katya looked at his bent head, saying nothing,
wanting to kiss him but sensing that he needed to
unburden himself.

'When I met you—well, you know what happened

when I met you. You were everything I'd ever imagined no woman could be: you were intelligent and gentle, funny and kind, responsive . . .' He curled her fingers into the palms of her hands, holding them fiercely between both of his own. 'I used to go home alone after I'd said good night to you and lie in bed and dream about that response of yours, my love. There was just one problem, or rather, I thought there was one problem. In fact, of course, there were two.' He fell silent.

'Vonnie?' she prompted in a small voice.

'She was the one I knew about. She'd hurt Dad badly. She'd abandoned Tom.'

'Tom?'

He lifted the hooded eyes swiftly. 'Yes, didn't you realise Tom is Dad's son? I arranged for him to be adopted by the couple that run his house in San Diego. They're wonderful people. And when Dad came out of the clinic and was ready to face the world again, Tom was there. I think in the long run, that's probably what kept him on the rails,' Matt added reflectively.

Katya raised his hand to her lips, kissing the palm and cradling it against her cheek wordlessly.

'Anyway, it was going to hurt Dad if I turned up madly in love with the cousin of his Princess Irena.'

'I could feel something like that,' Katya said softly. 'Sometimes you would look at me as if you wondered how you'd ever got mixed up with me. As if you disliked me.'

'Never that,' Matt returned swiftly, 'never. Not even in the worst times.'

'But you could be so cold. I thought I wasn't sophisticated enough,' Katya said, 'and you got impatient with me.'

'I got impatient with *me*. I wanted you so much and I knew it wasn't sensible,' said Matt, dropping his cheek against her hair.

She said, 'So you decided to be sensible and go back to Steffy Solomon.' It hurt.

His hands tightened. He tipped her face up towards him. 'Go back to Steffy?' he echoed blankly.

'You'd been involved with her before,' she muttered.

'No I hadn't. Oh, I was with her at that reception where we met, I agree, but that was just for the sake of the publicity. Steffy is not at all the sort of girl I'd voluntarily spend my free time with,' he said with more truth than chivalry.

Katya was bewildered. 'But she got you the job writing that film score for the Columbus film. You said you didn't want it but you couldn't hurt her feelings and turn it down.' She remembered so vividly; it had been almost the first twist of jealousy that he had cost her and she had hated it.

Matt began to laugh. 'You're way off beam, my love. *Columbus* was my Dad's idea. He's an executive these days as well as superannuated heart-throb, and he likes to promote my career when he can. It was *his* feelings I couldn't hurt. I shouldn't think Steffy's got any.'

'But you've been seen with her since.'

'So I should hope,' said Matt with feeling, 'that was the point of taking her out. A point, I may say, agreed between her agent and mine.'

Katya said, 'You said there were two problems, though. If Steffy wasn't the other one, what was?'

'You, my darling,' said Matt soberly. 'Or rather your damned innocence. You didn't know what I was all about, did you? And there I was, trying every way I could think of to *show* you that I loved you and this was for ever. You just kept fending me off as if I was some kind of slick Romeo after a one-night stand. I used to get pretty bitter about that, I can tell you.'

Katya said in a low, ashamed voice, 'I'm sorry.'

He sighed. 'I don't suppose it was all your fault.

I've known too many ladies in my time and I didn't realise you could be that different. I was bewildered. And then—when you met me at the airport—it seemed as if suddenly you understood and it was all going to come right.' His voice shook. 'Only it didn't, did it? The whole thing exploded in my hands. It was a disaster. And I couldn't understand *why*.'

It was a cry from the heart. It was also a question.

'I don't think I know why,' Katya said at last, slowly. 'I was afraid,' and as he flinched she added swiftly, 'oh, not of you; of the way you made me feel, perhaps. And though I was completely inexperienced, I wasn't ignorant. I'd watched Vonnie, I knew what falling in love could do to people. She's had some appalling misery, you know, no matter what you think of her. I was afraid that I would be the same. My grandfather always said we were alike. I was terrified of being hurt like her, becoming like her.'

Matt said, 'I didn't realise.'

'No, I don't suppose you did. You must always have thought of her as the villainess in your father's story, I can see that,' Katya said fairly. 'But I've seen her much more as a victim: of my grandparents, partly, but also of her own nature. I began to wonder if mine was the same.'

He stroked her cheek with the backs of his fingers. 'Why?'

Her lashes flicked up in a quick, half-shamed glance, and down again. 'Because of the way you made me feel, I suppose. Especially when you said that you didn't believe in romantic conventions and you'd never been in love. I thought you were offering me a straightforward trade of bodies, and I was scared,' she swallowed but went on bravely, 'because I wanted it.'

'Oh, my love,' Matt exclaimed remorsefully, 'why didn't you tell me?'

'How could I?' she asked simply. 'When I thought you didn't care?'

'Didn't care! My God, you had me on my knees,' he said between a laugh and a groan.

'That's not what you said. Or anyone else for that matter,' she added remembering Jack's warning in the woods on the day of the picnic.

'Well, the whole world knows different now,' said Matt grimly. 'Haven't you been reading my reviews? The critics have been positively gloating. "At last real feeling from Saracen". "Purified by suffering",' he quoted in disgust. 'Every damned interview I've given I've been asked whether I'm in love or the grip of a fatal disease.'

Katya looked at him gravely. 'What did you say?'

The mobile mouth twisted. 'That I didn't see much difference between the two.' His eyes took on a haunted, brooding look. 'After that day you threw me out I was in despair. I'd wanted to love you so much, and I ended up savaging you.'

'No!' protested Katya instinctively.

Matt was not to be comforted. 'Oh yes, I did. Don't try whitewashing. I knew I'd shocked you, I was pretty sure I'd hurt you. I was terrified I'd spoiled everything. In my worst nightmares I even began to wonder—well, afterwards I was scared to see you in case I hurt you again, made you frigid or something.'

Katya saw self-loathing in his face and was filled with compassion. 'Matt,' she said, taking his hands firmly in her own and shaking them, 'Matt, listen to me. You never hurt me, and you didn't do anything I didn't want you to do.'

He looked at her doubtfully.

'Honestly,' she said, 'I was shy and you were a super-sophisticate and I lost my cool. For which I cursed myself afterwards. That's all.' She gave him a slow, loving smile. 'When we made love in London, did it seem to you then that I had become frigid?'

He chuckled. 'I wasn't thinking too clearly, but no, not from what I recall.'

Katya sighed dreamily. 'I remember.'

'But then you went and left me *again*!' Matt's hands fell away and he sat back looking at her with mock despair. 'After I'd taken my heart out, dusted it down—even put it under the shower for you, dammit—and presented it to you with due ceremony. And you get up and creep away the next morning without even saying thank you nicely.' His voice cracked, in spite of the flippancy. 'Or even goodbye.'

'I thought you were scoring,' Katya told him, 'that it was a sort of revenge. You said you were proud of yourself.'

Matt looked at her speechlessly for a long moment. Then he thrust both hands through his hair in a gesture of absolute disbelief.

'Did I say you were intelligent? I withdraw it. I withdraw it utterly. Of course I was proud of myself. I'd got you to listen to me. I'd shown you in the most eloquent way I could that I loved you. We were magic together. I thought you felt it too—it couldn't have been like that if I'd just been taking some petty revenge, for God's sake. And anyway, what sort of man do you think I am?'

She leaned forward contritely and stopped his mouth with her own. 'I'm sorry, I'm sorry, I'm *sorry*,' she said against his lips. 'It's because I didn't know enough about any men, nice or nasty. It was my damned innocence, as you said. I'll do something about it.'

'Possibly,' said Matt releasing himself and running his hands up under her dark hair, letting it fall over his fingers in fascinated delight, 'but only under my expert tutelage and guidance. I am not letting you loose on an unsuspecting world.'

Katya was trembling. She did her best to disguise the effect that his touch had on her, however, putting her head on one side enquiringly. 'Oh?'

'Definitely. Can't have dynamite like you lying around loose.'

'I am not,' she stated, her eyes locking with his and her breath coming fast, 'loose.'

The grey eyes glinted with amusement and so much more that she was almost fainting with the intensity of it. 'Yes you are,' he contradicted, 'but not for much longer. I'm going to marry you and save the world.'

Katya's heart did a backward flip so that she almost gasped out loud. She was not, however, going to give him the satisfaction of realising this.

So, 'What if I don't want to marry you?' she asked politely.

A slow smile curled the sensuous mouth. 'I shall persuade you,' announced Matt. 'I shall enjoy that.'

She sniffed. 'I'm not very persuadable.'

'You will be.'

'You're very sure of yourself,' she teased, mock-offended.

'Yup. I've got a good battery of weapons.' He was laughing at her, but there was an underlying purpose that had her melting already. He leaned forward, touching his mouth to her skin in butterfly kisses that made her catch her breath. 'This. And serenades. I've been writing music for you, my love, I'll play you some of it tonight. And this,' he touched his tongue to her inner lip. 'And marriage. And undying love.'

Katya moved in his arms. 'You love me?' she asked in a little voice.

Matt's arms tightened. She had never felt so precious or beloved in her life. 'I love you so much,' he told her with fierce self-mockery, 'that I went and stood outside that damned apartment building this morning just to *see* the bloody place again and remember you. And then I saw you come out.'

She said, 'I see. So you had no idea that I was in Paris until then?'

'No. And presumably my passionate pleas for love— or at least some sort of explanation—have been used to light your grandparents' fire,' he said with the tolerance of a man who has won. 'But I didn't know how you might feel about me after all this time without a word, so I thought I'd better do something dramatic to get you to my side. I didn't fancy a broken leg, so hitting the bottle seemed the most convenient. I convinced everyone, too.'

'You—are—unprincipled,' Katya told him, impressed.

'Mmm. You are delicious.' His kisses were growing more urgent. 'Are you going to marry me?'

'Yes,' said Katya without hesitation, meeting his mouth hungrily, melting against him.

'And not mind the travelling? You'll go with me where I go?'

'Always.' She was twisting under his stroking hands.

'And trust me? Not believe gossip any more?'

'Never.' Her steaming raincoat and damp skirt were being gently prised away from her.

'And love me?'

Katya gave a little groan. 'I've already told you that.'

'You did?'

'On that night that you lured me into your house by underhand means,' she pointed out.

'So I did.' His mouth was moving over her exposed skin. She gave a little shiver of absolute pleasure.

'Matt, do you realise you have just taken off *all* my clothes?' she said at last, half-laughing, drenched in exquisite feeling.

'Well, of course,' he sounded surprised. 'You can't go to a concert by the famous Matthew Saracen in a scruffy raincoat and your working clothes.'

'I see,' she said ironically. 'Thank you for pointing it out to me. I wasn't intending to go to your concert when I came here this evening, though.'

He was shocked. 'You weren't?'

'I had a ticket,' she admitted, 'but I left it behind.'

He kissed her swiftly, wickedly on her parted lips while he ran his hands distractingly along the length of her thigh.

'Then what did you come here to do?' he whispered.

She gave him as cool a look as, in the circumstances, she could manage.

'I was assured I was needed to save your career. If not your life,' she told him.

'Ah. Well, in that case I should stop worrying,' he advised her blithely. 'You're perfectly dressed for saving my life.'

And after that she had neither the breath nor the wish to protest further.

You can keep this one
plus 4 free novels

Janet Dailey
Americana

Don't miss a single title from this great collection. The first eight titles have already been published. Complete and mail this coupon today to order books you may have missed.

Harlequin Reader Service

In U.S.A.
901 Fuhrmann Blvd.
P.O. Box 1397
Buffalo, N.Y. 14140

In Canada
P.O. Box 2800
Postal Station A
5170 Yonge Street
Willowdale, Ont. M2N 6J3

Please send me the following titles from the Janet Dailey Americana Collection. I am enclosing a check or money order for $2.75 for each book ordered, plus 75¢ for postage and handling.

_____	ALABAMA	Dangerous Masquerade
_____	ALASKA	Northern Magic
_____	ARIZONA	Sonora Sundown
_____	ARKANSAS	Valley of the Vapours
_____	CALIFORNIA	Fire and Ice
_____	COLORADO	After the Storm
_____	CONNECTICUT	Difficult Decision
_____	DELAWARE	The Matchmakers

Number of titles checked @ $2.75 each = $_____

N.Y. RESIDENTS ADD
  APPROPRIATE SALES TAX $_____

Postage and Handling $ .75

                    TOTAL $_____

I enclose _____

(Please send check or money order. We cannot be responsible for cash sent through the mail.)

PLEASE PRINT

NAME _____

ADDRESS _____

CITY _____

STATE/PROV. _____